Table of Contents

Through The Keyhole

An Erotic Collection of Short Stories
By Candy Caine

Visit Candy Caine at: http://www.candycaine.com[1]

Warning: This e-book contains sexually explicit content which is only suitable for mature readers

---

1.   http://www.candycaine.com/

DEVIL OR ANGEL

By
Candy Caine

I parked my car and checked the address Diana had given me, once more. The swanky building across the street had to be it. On a nurse's salary, I figured she must cut corners to afford the rent. I went inside and was greeted by a uniformed doorman.

"Good evening, Sir. May I help you?"

"I'm here to visit Diana Golden."

"One moment please," he said, stepping around his desk to the phone.

I watched him discreetly speak into the phone and replace it in its holder. "Just take the elevator to the top floor."

I thanked him and proceeded toward the elevator. The elevator was quick and opened onto a floor with only one door. Was this a penthouse apartment, I wondered as I approached the door. I was about to knock when I noticed the door was ajar. I guessed it had something to do with the surprise Diana had mentioned, as if seeing this apartment wasn't surprise enough. Pushing the door open, I went inside, but stopped dead in my tracks when I heard, "Get down on your knees, slave!" followed quickly by the unmistakable sound of a whip slapping flesh. At first I thought the voice was coming from a skin flick on the TV. Not that my sweet Diana would ever watch such stuff. But, when the voice commanded, "Closer, bitch!" I realized it *was* Diana. And that, I found *totally* unbelievable.

I would know—I'd been dating Diana for nearly three months. As far as I was concerned, she was an angel. Kind, gentle, and always ready to help someone. In fact, when I first opened my eyes in the hospital after being involved in a nasty auto accident, her beautiful, angelic face, with its smooth café au lait skin, finely sculptured high cheek bones and smiling soft brown, doe eyes, was the first thing I'd seen. And she wasn't only a pretty face.

As she bent over me to dab at the perspiration on my brow, my eyes fell to the rise of her ample breasts swelling above her bra. She wore a fresh scent that reminded me of a rose garden. I felt a stirring in my groin letting me know at least that part of my anatomy was still in working order.

I remember trying to lift my head, but the room began to swim around me. "Whoa...when did I get on the merry-go-round?"

"You have a bad concussion. You'll feel much better if you don't try to get up."

She had a sweet soothing voice and such gentle, caring hands. Seeing her was what made my short stay in the hospital tolerable.

That tender scene in my memory was rudely pushed aside when I heard Diana distinctly command, "Pleasure me, bitch!"

I followed the sounds to a bedroom and peered through a half-opened door. When my brain translated what my eyes saw, I stood there rooted to the floor in shock.

Diana was dressed in an outrageous outfit of black leather and latex. She wore a garter belt with fishnet stockings and leather boots with six-inch spiked heels that looked lethal. I couldn't miss the ugly, thick, metal studded collar around her slender neck. She wore black leather gloves and held a nasty-looking whip. A skintight latex corset with cutouts for her breasts finished off the outfit. One of her long legs rested on a chair exposing her pussy. Her black hair was loose and wild-looking, while her lips were like two blood-red gashes surrounding her mouth. She hardly resembled the sweet Diana I knew and loved.

On all fours on the floor in front of her was a dark-haired woman wearing only pink garters and fishnet stockings. Around her neck was a thick, spiked dog collar that was attached to a leash. Her more than ample bare ass bore a patchwork of angry red stripes.

"That's it slave, make me come."

I watched as the woman licked and sucked Diana's clit. The expression on Diana's face was sheer, self-absorbed pleasure. Suddenly, I found myself being turned on. So this was the big surprise, Diana had been hinting at. Yeah, it was a *real* surprise, all right—a shock was more like it.

My mind reeled back to the other night as we cuddled in the afterglow of our sweet lovemaking. We had met at a motel centrally located between both our jobs. "Let's do something different next Saturday," she'd said.

"Like what?" I asked, open for suggestions.

Her face brightened and a secretive smile completed the transformation.

"What?"

Her smile grew. And so did my curiosity. But all she said was, "Come to my place on Saturday night."

"What do you have in mind?" I asked, really wanting to know at this point.

"It's a surprise," she'd said with a mischievous glint in her eye.

I gave her my best *please tell me or I'll die look*, but it didn't work. Finally she ended the conversation with, "If I told you, it wouldn't be a surprise now, would it?"

Presently, as I stood rooted to the ground like some peeping Tom, my thoughts were racing. Why hadn't I detected this side of Diana? Half of me was repelled by what I saw, while the other half of was terribly aroused. Maybe I should turn around and just get out of here. A tiny voice in the back of my head told me it would be the right thing to do. However, it was my cock straining painfully against my jeans that had the deciding vote, silencing that tiny voice of reason.

I'd been so deep in thought; I hadn't realized Diana was staring at me. She'd probably known I'd been there all the time and had put on the little show for my benefit. However, I wasn't prepared to become part of the act. Therefore, when she barked an order at me, she took me by surprise.

"Get those clothes off!" she commanded.

Because I hadn't realized the order was directed at me, I didn't react at first. An angry sounding, "Now!" roused me to action. I took off my leather jacket and nearly freaked when I heard her say, "Show me your big cock."

Diana would never speak to me like that. I felt strange—this entire scene was becoming way too weird. I couldn't fathom how I could be feeling both aroused and yet felt so...vulnerable. Especially now that Diana had kicked the kneeling woman to the side and was giving me her *undivided* attention.

As my jeans hit the floor and I stepped out of them, Diana ordered the other woman to look at me. When she didn't obey quickly enough, Diana grabbed a handful of her hair and yanked her head up.

"Look how big and hard his cock is. You want to have it inside of you, don't you?"

In a small, trembling voice, the dark-haired woman replied, "Ye...yes, Mistress."

Diana's eyes were cold, hard green stones, yet they burned right through me when she told me to put my penis in the other woman's mouth. I was still half-wondering if I was dreaming and hesitated. I also hesitated because deep-down inside I knew this would be the last chance I had to split before I got in over my head. Diana didn't like that one bit. I was still arguing with myself when the decision was taken away from me. With unbelievable speed and agility, she whipped my buttocks. "You dare defy me?"And then she whipped me again.

It was weird. Though my ass stung like a son of a gun, I was completely turned on. That little voice in the back of my head hadn't just been squashed, it had been obliterated. I was ready to obey. The other woman took me into her mouth greedily and began to suck me clear up to my balls. It was incredible. I knew at this rate I'd be spewing soon.

"Suck his cock, bitch! Suck it while I fuck your sweet, tight pussy," Diana commanded.

Diana had strapped on a nasty-looking, black dildo and began to fuck the other woman from behind. As a result, the woman began to work my rod harder and faster. I let loose a groan, pulling her closer to me. The girl's long tongue slurped over my tip and my balls, hitting my sensitive spot behind them. Then she'd take all of me into that talented mouth of hers as if she were a vacuum cleaner.

Diana must have sensed I was about to climax because she shouted at me. "Don't you dare come! You will not ejaculate until I give you permission."

My eyes met her glare and my body froze in response as if a bucket of icy water had been dropped on my cock. My throat tightened as my organ shriveled. The other woman continued to suck me, but my cock had all but died and given up the ghost.

"Halt slave!" Diana ordered. Then with the tip of her whip she nudged me. "You position yourself behind her."

I complied with Diana's wishes and went to stand in back of the kneeling woman.

"You may come inside the slave."

I grabbed the sides of the woman's ass which was still flaming red from Diana's whip. She was so wet that her juices had already begun to run down the insides of her thighs. I slipped inside with ease and began to move, slowly.

"Harder!" Diana commanded. "Pound that bitch! Punish her with your cock!"

I began to slam into her and my cock grew hard instantly. Sweat began to bead across my forehead. Before long, it began to slowly seep into my eyes. I wiped them away as best as I could. I'd never fucked a woman this hard for fear it might hurt her, but hell, it was a thrilling feeling. All I heard was the smacking of my balls against the slave's ass as I rammed into her. I was enjoying this and wanted it to last as long as it could.

The woman moaned in pleasure and tried to meet my every thrust. She reached underneath herself and rubbed her clit in order to heighten her own pleasure. I grabbed one of her swaying breasts and began to knead its nipple between my thumb and forefinger. That drew another moan from her. She put her hand over mine and squeezed it. I heard the message loud and clear and increased the pressure on her nipple. It wasn't enough, so I eventually pulled on it. She really liked that and within moments I felt her begin to tremble with an orgasm. I continued what I was doing until I felt her last spasm. Then I grabbed her hips, thrusting as fast as I could until I exploded and shot hot come into her.

Talk about weird. Ten minutes later, Diana had slipped out of her gear and put on a bathrobe, while the dark-haired woman threw on some sweats. I got back into my clothes, as well. Then we all sat around the kitchen table cooling off with cold beers. It was as if Diana's evil twin sister had gone back to the dungeon she'd escaped from.

"John, this is Ann," she said matter-of-factly. "We work together at the hospital.

"This is really some place," I said, still overwhelmed with her apartment.

"It's a terrific find. I can make as much noise as I like without disturbing the neighbors."

"How long have you been doing...this?" I asked Diana.

"Five years."

"Wow! I would have never guessed."

"Did you enjoy yourself?" Ann asked.

She spoke with a slight Hispanic accent. I realized I hadn't really heard her speak before. Remembering her angry-looking ass, I threw the question right back at her. "Did *you?*"

She gave me a smile. "Of course. I always do."

"Would you like to do this again some time?" Diana asked me.

"I dunno. I found it kinda…intense."

"I think you do," Diana said quietly. "You probably never climaxed before like you just did."

She had me there. My orgasm had been unbelievable. But, that domination thing. Ann had been the one getting whacked. How would I feel if I were in her place?

"What do you say? Are you game?" Diana interrupted my thoughts.

"Okay, but…"

"What's on your mind?"

"I was thinking about us—"

"You and me?"

"Yeah. How will that affect us—the relationship we now have?"

"It doesn't have to unless you decide to change it."

"I honestly don't see how it can remain the same."

"It can. You'll see. Trust me."

Trust her, she said. Even though I wasn't really certain how that might be possible, I agreed, anyway, to another session with Lady Di, the moniker she went by in the trade. No matter what, the sex I'd had with those two women had been the hottest I'd ever experienced. I soon began to look forward to the next session.

Thinking about this, I had to wonder. Had Diana tapped into some masochistic streak I never knew I possessed? How the hell could pain be so inviting, I'd absolutely no idea. All I knew was that I craved more of the same. And I couldn't think of anything else until the next time.

***

When I met Diana for dinner during the weekend, my misgivings about the domination hurting our relationship were tempered, but not altogether removed. Certainly when we went back to my place and made love, it was tender and sweet with me being the initiator, but I still felt weird about it. Perhaps because it was lurking in the back of my mind, I couldn't help wondering if Diana was someone with multi-personalities. While we were together, I had no qualms about our relationship. Her lips and arms were as sincere as they were before I discovered her secret life. I felt such contentment as we lay cuddled together afterwards. It was only after she was gone that the doubt would surface.

***

The night I was supposed to go to Diana's, I was more than just a little nervous. In fact, I almost chickened out and called to cancel. However, a delightful flashback of that fantastic climax stopped me from doing so. When I knocked on Diana's door, she opened it, already wearing her dominatrix costume.

"Right on time, slave. Good. Go directly to the bedroom."

As soon as I reached the bedroom, she commanded me to strip. Then she handed me an ugly-looking black latex mask. I noticed it had holes for my nose, but zippers were placed where the eyes and mouth were.

"A little early for Halloween," I said, immediately regretting it.

She cruelly grabbed my crotch and squeezed. "Rule number one: Do not speak unless asked to. Now put that mask on."

I was *not* expecting that and Lord, did it hurt! It took a few moments for the throbbing to subside. And I assure you, following that, I did what I was told. The mask was hot and smelly, but at least the zippers were open so I could see.

"On your knees," Diana commanded next.

I got down on all fours and allowed her to put a dog collar around my neck. It had a large D-shaped ring to which she then attached a short leather leash. Similar cuffs were attached around my wrists and ankles.

Suddenly I began to get the feeling I'd made a *big* mistake. When Ann was the slave, it had been a better deal. Now as Diana was attaching all the potential restraints, I wasn't too certain I was going to like being the designated slave.

"Stand, slave."

My eyes opened wide when I saw what Diana had in her hands. Those dainty, delicate hands now held lethal-looking nipple clamps. Attaching them to my tender buds brought tears to my eyes, but at least I was able to stifle an unmanly yelp. If the tit clamps had been a shock, I nearly had a stroke when she slipped a cock ring around my balls and then worked it around my semi erect member. My poor cock didn't know what to do, waiting for some signal from my brain. However, I was too confused to think straight—half out of my mind with trepidation and half-excited with anticipation. A chain was then fastened from the cock ring to each of my nipples, which were now completely numb.

"Heel, slave!" Diana barked, tugging my leash.

She had me stand under a large hook suspended from the ceiling. "Raise your

arms over your head," Diana said. I stood there, arms suspended in air and watched as she carried over a stool to stand on. Dutifully, I allowed her to attach my wrists to the hook.

I felt like a slave on the block being checked out for sale as she walked around me admiring her handiwork before running her hands lightly over my goose-pimpled skin. The cock ring tightened as my cock responded. She flashed me a wicked smile which sent bad vibes spidering down my spine and a fluttering in my gut.

Now helpless, I watched bug-eyed as Diana chose a whip, with long nylon strands extending from the handle, from a rack of assorted whips.

"Now slave, pledge your obedience to me."

When I said nothing, she swung the whip hard against my ass. I could still feel the sting moments later.

Diana repeated. "Do you *understand?*"

"Yes," I heard a strange voice, I hardly recognized as my own, say.

That earned me another hard swipe with the whip. I hardly knew what the punishment was for. However, as much as it hurt, it turned me on. Unbelievable.

"The correct answer was yes, *Mistress.*"

I nodded yes, but saw her raise her hand. Correcting myself quickly, I replied, "Yes, Mistress."

"Good. Now listen carefully. "Rule number two: you will come *only* when I say you can. Is that understood?"

Staring at the whip in her hand, I said, "Yes, Mistress." I had no idea how hard it was going to be to obey this rule.

To my surprise, she began to whip me—everywhere! My brain couldn't comprehend why especially after I'd pledged my obedience. She struck my back, my ass, and the backs of my legs. Instead of fear, I felt aroused and wanted to come in the worst way. Besides, the cock ring was beginning to feel like a vise. I wondered what disobeying that rule would earn me. Something told me I didn't want to know, so I tried to wrap my mind around work—anything non-sexual. She continued to torture me with the whip a few more minutes before releasing me from the hook.

"Get down on all fours."

She grabbed the leather leash attached to the D-ring on my collar and walked me, like a dog, over to the bed.

"Lie down on the bed—face up."

She positioned me spread-eagled, attaching my wrists and ankles to chains on the four posts. She purposely reached over my body and brushed my face with her exposed tits to tease me. It worked. The cock ring had become uncomfortably snug again with my penis waving in the air.

From the night table, she picked up a large feather attached to a handle and a fur mitt. Diana knew how ticklish I was and was obviously going to use it as a form of torture.

She chose to use the feather first. Gently, barely touching my skin, she stroked it across my chest—back and forth. My nipples tightened into such hard pebbles, I feared they'd never soften again. After dwelling a few minutes, her attention dropped lower to my arms and legs. Over and over again she tormented me with that dam feather. I squirmed and pulled against my restraints. I was going crazy. And if she didn't stop, I was going to scream. Then when I thought it couldn't get worse, she stroked the most sensitive spot on my entire body—right behind my balls. Fearing I was going to lose it and let loose, I gasped and bit down on my bottom lip hard enough to draw blood.

Then, miraculously, she stopped. However it was only a short reprieve. She switched to a fur mitt and repeated the torture once more. I couldn't stand another stroke and cried out. I'd had enough of her teasing and desperately needed to touch her. More than that, I wanted to ram my cock right into her. She had reduced me to a blathering idiot and I was willing to beg—do practically anything at this point to get off.

That's when I learned her most important rule of all, number three: "I need to come—often." That meant her, *of course*.

Diana got on the bed and lowered her pussy to inches over my face. Close enough to smell her musky womanly aroma, but too far for my extended tongue to reach.

"Want me, slave?"

"Yes, Mistress."

"Good. Make me come."

She lowered herself close enough for me to reach her with my mouth. I alternately pulled and sucked her engorged clit with my lips before whipping my tongue across it. She was already wet and I thrust in and out, her essence smearing across my face as she gyrated her hips to meet my tongue thrusts. Then she became so hot, she practically smothered me by grinding her pussy into my face. I nearly couldn't lick or suck fast enough to keep up with her movements. I was able to bring her to climax quickly, but I'd become a ticking bomb close to coming myself. I watched her body tremble as the expression of her face changed to one of total absorption. When her orgasm was over, she slid down my chest to my straining cock, leaving a wet trail of her love juice in her wake.

Diana had to know how crazy she was making me. Even so, she continued the sweet torture by only grazing my cock with her wet pussy. I tried to raise my body from the bed in order to reach her, but to no avail. Finally, just as I thought I'd die, she stopped her teasing and lowered herself onto my straining rod. I filled her completely, emitting a sigh. But she still didn't give me permission to come. She knew she was tormenting me as she slowly moved up and down. I could detect a look of pure evil lust in her eyes. She was going well beyond the realm of torture. I wanted to explode right then and there, but feared breaking her damn rule. My feverish mind debated coming, anyway. Once I got off, I could stand whatever she dished out. One glance at the whip, though, and my thoughts of rebellion—and relief—were gone.

My agony was now off the charts and increased ten-fold as her movement began to pick up speed. I watched as her eyes closed and her face grew tight. I grit my teeth, thought of stuff as unrelated to sex as possible, trying in the worst way to control my ejaculation. She began to tremble as a soft moan passed her lips. Then she blessed me with the words I longed to hear the most. "You can now come."

However, before I could act on the order, she lifted off my cock and reversed her body changing the angle that my shaft was entering her pussy. It gave me a gorgeous view of her pussy lips and perfectly round ass. Since I wasn't able to touch her since I was still restrained, she did all the work. She began to move slowly. Just watching my cock move in and out of her was one of the most tantalizing sights in the entire world. Then she began to move faster and faster. That pushed me over the edge. I exploded inside her. My climax continued for minutes—longer than any I'd ever experienced before. It was so intense that my entire body shook.

Diana smiled. "Good slave. Here's your treat," she said turning around and lowering one of her luscious tits to my mouth. I suckled greedily. And found that I was getting aroused once more.

She undid my restraints and led me off the bed and out of the room into the kitchen of all places. I was pushed down into a chair and she straddled me. She began to move seductively slow at first, up my semi-hard cock and then down. I could feel my blood surging towards it and engorging it until I filled her completely. She soon moved faster, giving me permission to touch her tits which were bouncing through the cutouts in her vest.

I grabbed her nipples, tugging and fanning them with my fingers. She seemed to enjoy that and began to grind her bottom into me each time she came down. I suckled one nipple and then the other. She didn't seem to mind, so I wasn't punished for the infraction. She had one more orgasm and allowed me to come, as well. That last climax sapped whatever little strength I had left. Diana seemed just as exhausted.

"You may take off your mask, slave."

I did so and the cooler air in the room immediately started to dry my sweaty head. Next she began to remove all the rest of the hardware I was wearing.

"Well, what do you think?" she asked, in a non dominatrix tone of voice.

I had no words to describe what I'd just experienced.

"Would you like to do it again—with a different routine?"

"Yeah...I do."

Before tonight, I wouldn't have ever believed I'd be into that kind of stuff. But I knew I was hooked. I must have gone over to the *dark side* and man was it something.

"Good." She smiled. We set another date.

*****

Before long I'd become a true slave to Lady Di and my own crazy fantasies. I was addicted. Somehow the thin line between pleasure and pain had become merged. And I couldn't get enough of it. Despite all the domination, I still continued a normal relationship with Diana. The weirdest thing of all was that I wasn't certain which Diana I needed more.

Soon I began to live from session to session. I hardly missed the fact I was seeing Diana outside of them less and less. Of course, I told no one about my descent into the world of domination—not even Steve, the one guy at work I was closest to. We used to go out on Fridays looking for babes at the bars before I met Diana. He had been in the car with me the night of the accident and had badly broken his arm in the crash requiring surgery. After Diana came into the picture, we drifted apart.

Then out of the blue, Steve called me. He sounded upset and wanted to meet for a drink.

"Hey, John. Glad you came," he said, shaking my hand as I sat down.

He looked like hell. "What's up?" I asked.

There was a pitcher of beer on the table. I poured myself a glass as he began to talk.

"Do you remember the nurse you had while you were in the hospital?"

"Of course I do—"

"Well, we started to date and before long she pulled me into her world of domination. Can you believe that sweet, angelic lady was actually a dominatrix? Soon our normal dates became less frequent, but I didn't care. All I wanted was to be her love slave. Until I discovered she was videotaping our sessions and selling them. What's the matter, John, you look sick?"

Sick? I felt as if my entire world had imploded. A cold hand began to squeeze my heart as my throat constricted. I immediately got a sinking feeling my entire life as I once knew it was about to be flushed down a sewer of gossip and shame.

He looked at me a moment. "Don't tell me. Were you involved with Lady Di, also?"

I nodded.

"Oh, no. Not you, too. I wonder how many others."

"Do you think she taped my sessions, as well?" I asked.

"Probably. How the hell do you think she can afford that place or her fancy car?"

"Are you going to continue to see her?"

"I don't know," he said. "It's not like there's a Dominatrix Anonymous group to join."

So much for my angel of mercy, I thought.

-The End-

MY LOVER'S SECRET LIFE

By
Candy Caine

"By that smile on your face, you finally did it, didn't you?" my best friend, Tina, teased the minute I walked into the office lounge of Madsen and Dwyer, the advertising agency where we both worked as secretaries.

She'd certainly made the right call. I finally met the guy I'd been chatting with on the Internet for months. Our fears of ruining a great friendship if we met and it went sideways were laid to rest last night. We got the courage to take the plunge and meet at a bar on Third Avenue.

"Uh-huh."

"I guess Bernard wasn't a toad."

"Uh-uh."

"Tell me everything."

"Well...He's just gorgeous, with beautiful hazel eyes that I nearly drowned in and from the way his clothes fit, I think he has a great body, too." I smiled as I recalled more. "His black hair is not too short and he's got this thingee in the middle of his chin," I said, pointing to my own.

"A cleft?"

"Yeah. One of those. He's also got an adorable smile and he's quite a gentleman."

"So he held the door open for you and pulled out your chair. I wonder how long that will last," Tina replied.

I knew she was thinking about her last date, the guy she had called "Mr. Ego", so I cut her some slack. "Hey, not all guys are self-centered pricks, you know."

"Sorry, Jasmine. Didn't mean to rain on your parade. I'm glad things worked out between you and Bernard. When are you seeing him again?"

"Saturday." I looked at my watch. "Hey we've got to get back to our desks."

"See you later," Tina said, heading for the elevator.

***

I wished the week away. All I cared about was seeing Bernard again. Now that we'd met, chatting on the Internet couldn't cut it for me anymore.

Bernard showed up that Saturday in a navy-blue sports jacket and tan slacks. We went to a small restaurant for dinner and later to a club to dance. He turned the heads of every woman we passed and a few men, too, but all his attention seemed to be focused on me. What a great ego booster that was for me!

Over dinner, we talked and talked. You would think that after conversing over the Internet for so long we'd know everything there was to know about each other, but there was still so much to learn.

"I'm not really a native New Yorker," Bernard admitted. "I moved from a small town in Ohio when I was thirteen."

"Was your family large like mine?" I had mentioned to Bernard that I had three older brothers when he told me he taught Tae Kwan Do at a midtown gym. One of my brothers had taken Tae Kwan Do and was a black belt in judo.

"I was the youngest of six kids, and the only boy. My sisters treated me more like a Ken doll than a brother. I didn't wear any outfit for more than fifteen minutes."

I laughed. "If it's any consolation, I was the only girl in my family."

"Yeah, but did your brothers play with Barbie dolls?"

"No, thank God!"

The band began to play a mellow song. Bernard stood and offered me his hand. "Let's dance."

Dancing with Bernard was heavenly. Feeling his strong arms around my back was definitely a turn-on. Between the magical blend of his aftershave and unique male scent, I was becoming quite heady. Though everything about him shouted male, there seemed to be a softer side to him, which made me feel comfortable talking to him. I could say the things to him I would normally only tell Tina. I sensed that he was just the type of man I could fall in love with. He wasn't just a handsome cut-out. There was cake below the icing.

Unfortunately, time has a way of fleeting especially when you're enjoying yourself. We drove back to my apartment. Bernard took the key from me and opened the door. I walked inside and he followed me.

"Thanks for a wonderful evening, Bernard."

"I had a good time, too. How about a rerun next Saturday?"

"I'd love it."

"Good. I'll email you and we'll figure out something to do," he said, bending to kiss me good night.

The kiss had started out quite chaste, but quickly grew into a passionate one, leaving us both gasping for breath. We looked into each other's eyes and an instant later, he had lifted me up onto the small table in the hall, knocking everything on it to the floor. As his lips sought mine again, he reached under my skirt and pulled off my panties. Unzipping his fly, he pulled out his stiff rod and nudged it into my welcoming pussy. I gasped as he filled me. With my arms firmly around his neck, he pumped into me slowly at first, but our escalating needs made him quicken the pace. His left hand closed over my right breast. I could feel his fingers fan my nipple through the sheer material of my blouse. It was moments later that I heard myself moan in pleasure as the first spasm grabbed me and I started to come. Bernard nuzzled my neck and soon reached his own climax.

Bernard smiled down at me and whispered, "You were wonderful, baby."

"Hmm. That was right up there along with chocolate."

"Not as sweet as this," he said covering my mouth with his, rekindling the still glowing embers into flames once more. Having already met the urgency, he swept me up and carried me into the bedroom. We fell back together onto the bed and began to slowly undress one another.

Bernard and I began to make love again, but allowed ourselves to savor each kiss and every touch. We took the time to explore one another's bodies. I stroked his cock as he kissed my taut nipples, rousing them further into tight raisins. Slowly his hands moved downward, lightly skimming both sides of my body to my thighs. He explored my thighs a short time before moving back up to my stomach and kissed my navel. I put my arms around his neck as my lips sought his. We kissed deeply as our legs intertwined and we rolled over. Passion pounded the blood through me. I felt as if I was half ice and half fire. He kissed my neck and licked my ear. We rolled again. My body began to melt as my back arched involuntarily. I could feel my love juices pooling.

Bernard kissed his way down my body and stopped at my sex. Lifting my thighs, he brought my bottom closer to his mouth. He licked and sucked my clit, thrusting his tongue inside me as deep as it would go. My body began to twitch and buck as I was hurled into an explosion of pure delight.

When the last spasm of my climax ended, I pulled Bernard up and he slid easily into my slick pussy. Together we found the perfect tempo that bound our bodies together. A few minutes later, I heard him grunt and felt him stiffen momentarily before he came. He collapsed on top of me, his head on my chest. I stroked his back a few minutes before we both fell into a contented sleep.

After that weekend, we began to see each other exclusively. I couldn't be any happier since Bernard met my every need and then some. Aside from being the handsomest guy I ever dated, he was also the best lover. I couldn't believe how fortunate I was to have found a guy like him.

***

One night after dinner, a few months later, I was very restless and decided to drive over to Bernard's apartment and surprise him with dessert.

He was very glad to see me and made coffee. I cut the apple pie I'd brought and we sat down at the kitchen table. I have no idea what got into me that made me act so wanton, but I reached under the table and stroked Bernard's cock, which certainly got a rise out of him.

"Come here," he said, opening his arms. "You're the real dessert."

I didn't need to be asked twice as I slipped into his open arms and we kissed our way into his bedroom. His kisses had a unique way of stoking my fire and the anticipation of the pleasures to follow excited me even more. It was as if I could never get enough of this man.

As we began to undress one another, he suddenly pushed me away. I watch in surprise as he ran into the bathroom, slamming the door behind him. I feared that the pie hadn't agreed with him.

I rushed to the door and knocked. "Are you all right, Bernard?"

"Yeah, fine. Be out in a sec."

"Okay," I said, but I worried just the same.

"Now, where were we?" Bernard said, emerging from the bathroom, with a towel wrapped around his middle, acting as if nothing had happened.

Even though I felt relieved he wasn't ill, I still needed some enticing to get back into the mood. After all, I'd never seen him act so strangely.

Several minutes in his arms took care of that problem. His caress was like a match thrown on a pile of old newspapers. Heat and passion spread through my body like a wildfire. In moments, my clothes were strewn everywhere and Bernard was inside me.

The following morning, I opened my eyes to discover Bernard's side of the bed was empty. Wanting to go look for him, I went over to his bureau in search of a tee shirt to wear. I opened a drawer and found only socks. In another I found briefs. I felt I was getting warm, so I opened still another drawer. I nearly died right there on the spot.

The drawer was filled with fancy, silk women's lingerie. Who did this stuff belong to? Was it a collection of all Bernard's conquests? With anger welling within me and growing, I went to check the closet for other women's things. Hanging inside I found several slinky-looking dresses with matching shoes. What man keeps the clothes of a woman he's broken up with? Or...maybe...he was still seeing them. That last thought chilled me to the bone. I'd thought he was dating only me.

I turned as I heard Bernard walking into the bedroom. He was holding a breakfast tray. He must have realized what I'd been doing and that I had discovered his secret, because a moment later, a look of sheer horror appeared on his face.

"You found the clothes, didn't you?"

"Yes."

"It's not what you think, you know."

"How do you know what I'm thinking?"

"They're mine."

"What did you say?" I cocked my head.

"The clothes belong to me. I wear them."

"Terrific! I'm out of here," I said, gathering my things and fleeing into the bathroom.

"Jasmine, baby girl, I can explain."

"What's there to explain? You're some kind of pervert and I can't deal with that right now."

"I'm not gay."

"Fine. Now go away and let me dress in peace."

"Or a bi-sexual, either."

" That's nice. I don't care."

"Jasmine, please..."

"Go away, damnit!"

I realized that I probably wasn't thinking rationally or being very fair. But, I was reeling with the fact that the man I loved, with all my heart, wasn't as macho and virile as I'd thought, but some sick weirdo, instead. It was just too much for me to bear at the moment. I finished dressing and wanted to get out of there as quickly as possible. I needed time to sort this all out. Bernard tried to stop me, but I was in no mood to listen to whatever twisted explanation he'd planned to tell me.

Crying all the way home, it was a wonder I got there at all. I was upset and angry, but I wasn't sure with whom. Was I so blindly in love that I missed the signals Bernard gave out? Or what? I just didn't get it. He was so manly looking and a fantastic lover. Damnit! If he wasn't gay, as he said, what was he? Bisexual? No. He said he wasn't. Then...a transvestite or cross-dresser?

My mind wandered back to when I was a kid growing up. I recalled the terrible stories about the boy who lived down the block from my family. He liked to dress like a girl, too. People used to make fun of him and call him horrid names. He was beaten up all the time at school. Eventually his family moved away. If Bernard wasn't sure who or what he was, how could I be?

When I opened the door to my apartment, the phone was ringing off the hook. I knew it had to be Bernard, so I turned off the ringer. I had no intention of answering any of his e-mail, either. Not seeing him anymore was probably the best thing. Cut it off now before things got worse, I told myself. If breaking up was best, why was I so miserable just thinking about it?

I found it hard to sleep that night. Every time I closed my eyes, I saw Bernard's handsome face and felt his lips kissing mine. God, how I missed him, already! But I didn't need his craziness or whatever it was, to complicate my life.

Bernard had left dozens of messages on my computer. I deleted them all without reading a single one.

The following day flowers were delivered to my office with a note attached that read, "Please talk to me, I love and need you, Bernard."

"You guys have a knocked-down dragged-out fight, or something?" Tina asked when she saw me. "You look like crap."

"Thanks for the compliment. It wasn't exactly an argument."

"Well, what happened?"

"We broke up. He's perverted."

"What?"

"He wears women's clothes. And God only knows what else."

"Did you talk to him about this?"

"No way!"

"Why not?"

"Because, I didn't want to get involved. It would be hideous, just like the kid down the block."

"You totally lost me. Who's the kid down the block and what does he have to do with Bernard?"

I sighed and collapsed into a chair. "I knew you wouldn't understand."

"I might if you made some sense."

"When I was a kid, there was a boy that lived a few houses down from me who dressed in girl's clothes, too. His poor family was practically run out of town."

"I don't think that will be the same problem here. Bernard doesn't do it in public, does he?"

"No, I don't think so."

"How did you find out about this?"

"I found the stuff in his dresser drawer and closet."

"If you hadn't opened that drawer, would you have known?"

"No, I guess not."

"So you decided to trash your relationship without even talking about it?"

"I knew you wouldn't understand..."

"You think because I disagree with the way you're acting I don't understand?"

I turned away in a feeble attempt to try and control the tears filling my eyes.

"Are you afraid he might be gay or bisexual? Is that why you refuse to deal with this?"

When I didn't answer, Tina said, "Just as I thought. You're a fool."

"Why don't you mind your own business?"

"Great idea. When you come to your senses and want to talk like a rational human being, look me up. Until then, have a nice life, Jasmine," Tina, said, and walked away.

I spoke to no one for the rest of the day. I stayed by myself, miserable and reveling in it. When it was finally time to go home, I left without saying goodbye to a soul.

Walking towards my car, suddenly Bernard stepped out in front of me, blocking my way.

"Go away!"

"Not until you talk to me."

"I have nothing to say."

"I won't let you throw our love away."

I turned away, not wanting him to see the tears welling in my eyes.

"What we had was terrific. How can you just trash it?"

"Look, I can't talk about this now."

"Then when? Don't forget, in this country you're innocent until proven guilty. At least hear me out."

"No Bernard, no matter what you say, nothing will change the awful way I'm feeling right now."

"Fine. Hopefully, you'll come to your senses and change your mind. If you want to talk, you know where to find me," he said, tears in his eyes.

He raised his hand to my cheek, gently touched it, and was gone. Not wanting him to see me cry, I bit my bottom lip so hard that it began to bleed leaving a bitter taste in my mouth.

***

As the days passed into weeks, I didn't feel any better about my decision. In fact, I refused to think about it. But I did miss Bernard, more and more as time passed. There was a hole in my heart that refused to heal. No one understood why I couldn't deal with his perversion, especially Tina, who had written me off. She felt I'd overreacted and didn't give Bernard a fair shake. I soon began to feel as if I was the crazy one.

Eating dinner one night, a few weeks later, I opened one of the several magazines I subscribe to, but hardly find the time to read. I thumbed through it and found an article written by the wife of a cross-dresser, of all people. I began to read the article, which turned out to be a real eye-opener. By the time I finished reading I had an entirely different outlook on the subject of cross-dressing.

If I understood what the woman said, cross-dressers like Bernard were merely expressing the softer, more feminine side of their personalities. It didn't mean that they were gay or bisexual. I began to suspect that I might have truly overreacted out of ignorance and condemned Bernard without giving him a chance to defend himself. Ultimately, I'd stereotyped Bernard and tarred him with the same brush of hateful ignorance that homophobes use. And I had been the one who loved him. What made matters worse, was that I still did. I guess I gave new meaning to "you really hurt the one you love". But, the big question was whether or not I'd be able to accept his cross-dressing behavior.

I dropped the magazine, dumped my dinner dishes into the sink, and headed over to my computer. I began to surf the Internet trying to learn as much as I could about cross- dressing. I couldn't believe how many support groups there were out there. The more I read about the subject, the more miserable I became. I wanted a guarantee that whatever decision I made would be the right one, but I didn't possess the wisdom of the ages or a crystal ball. Instead, I realized that all I had to go on was how I felt inside. I had already discovered that I couldn't live without Bernard. Not a day passed without me thinking about him, wondering how he was or what he was doing. Not having a clue left me so wretched and depressed. Could I live with him and his cross-dressing? I wasn't going to find that out standing in my kitchen.

As the thought of going to Bernard's apartment entered my conscious brain, my heart began to hammer inside my chest just thinking of how it had felt to be held in his loving arms. And when the warm flow of desire began to course through my body, I took that as a pretty good indication that what I was about to do was the right thing. I grabbed my coat, purse, and rushed out of the apartment.

As I drove, I suddenly thought that maybe I should have called Bernard first. What if he wasn't home or had another woman there? If he was with someone, I'd certainly feel like a fool. But then, it would be truly over, wouldn't it? I sighed. I'd just have to gamble.

I knocked on his door, my heart pounding nearly as loud. I had to talk to him...at least to apologize. The door opened.

"Jasmine!"

Instantly I was in Bernard's arms, his lips covering mine. I didn't care what was right or wrong as he lifted me in his strong arms and carried me into the bedroom. His lips were everywhere as he began to regain his possession of my body.

"I love you, Jasmine," Bernard whispered, as he kissed my hair, eyes and finally, my waiting mouth. His tears of joy mingled with mine. And in that moment, as his lips devoured mine, I realized I'd been a fool. If our love were meant to be, it would transcend every obstacle along the way. I only had to believe that. I would make every conscious effort to understand him and accept his needs. I loved him.

Afterward, as we cuddled together, we talked. Bernard never wore feminine clothes outside of the apartment. No one had to know or would know, unless one of us told them. At that moment, I knew I wanted Bernard more than anything and somehow we'd be okay.

"You know there's a silver-lining in all this, Jasmine."

I looked up at him, curious.

"You're not my size, baby girl."

I immediately understood what he meant and laughed. "Wait until I'm pregnant. Then I'll be wearing *your* stuff."

"What's mine is yours," he said, and kissed me.

-The End-

Oops!

By
Candy Caine

Halfway into my second Cosmopolitan, I noticed her sizing me up. Strange, I thought, why would an African-American chick be interested in me? Last time I checked, I was a white, strawberry-blonde *female*—with freckles. Usually, I attracted a guy looking to score, not some pretty woman with large almond eyes. My interest peaked, I glimpsed at her from the corner of my eye. She had high cheekbones, which gave her an exotic look, and full lips—the kind many women would pay big bucks to have. Her glossy, dark-brown hair was short and spiked, but on her, it looked sexy. She was one helluva eye-fetching package.

A small impish smile played across her full lips as if she knew I was watching her watch me. This entire scenario made no sense, at all—unless I'd ventured into a gay bar. However, a quick glance at the other patrons didn't support the theory, so I continued to sip my drink, gearing up for the next one. I wanted to obliterate the ugly scene, which clung to my memory, like fleas on a dog. It had me getting sloshed every night to help get me through the endless hours.

Even now, I could close my eyes and still see Jeremy holding the redhead's long legs wide apart as he rammed his love stick into her like a jack knife. The guy who'd professed to desire only me. Yeah, right. He probably meant *when I was with him.* As I watched that carnal spectacle, I began to wonder how many other women he'd screwed in our bed? It wouldn't have been so traumatic had I not been in this position before. Damn! Are all men natural-born cheats or do I keep picking the same kind of dog, whose vocabs lacked words like *faithful* and *honesty?*

Her sidling off the bar stool yanked me from my thoughts. She was taller than I'd imagined her to be as she walked towards me; her leather mini skirt hardly concealed her long, creamy-beige, shapely legs.

As she slipped onto the stool next to me, she purred, "You look like you need a friend."

"And you're James Taylor, right?"

She cocked a perfectly arched eyebrow as I made reference to one of Taylor's old songs, *You've Got a Friend.*

"Actually, I'm doing real fine on my own," I said.

"Really? So why are you teary-eyed and getting tanked?"

"Who are you, Dr. Phil in drag?"

She gave out a throaty chuckle. "I'm better."

"How's that?" I asked, curious where this conversation was heading.

"Dr. Phil can never truly understand. You have to walk a mile in someone's shoes to really know the score."

My brain was way too pickled to have a heavy-duty psychological tête à tête at this point, but she kept talking.

"Nobody comes to a dump like this unless they want to forget," she said. "And, I think some man has done you dirty. Tell me I'm wrong."

I put my drink down and turned to face her. No doubt about it, she was a real knockout. "Give that girl a prize."

She gave me a smug smile which triggered my comeback. "So what?"

"Here's where we commiserate together," she replied.

What the hell, I was strung out enough to feel sorry for myself and began to unload on her. She turned out to be a real good listener. We'd both had another drink before she suggested I let her take me home.

***

The cool night air began to clear my head some and enough of my pistons were still firing for me to realize she'd taken me to her place. I stated the obvious.

"This isn't my apartment."

"I don't want to be alone tonight and I doubt you do, either, Sara."

She was right on the money, again. How could she be able to read me so well? I hoped she wasn't clairvoyant—or worse—a witch. I'd heard some nasty stories about witches. The last thing I needed now was for her to turn me into a nasty toad or turnip.

The walls of Deidre's small, neat apartment were covered with framed pictures of her wearing evening clothes and bikinis in front of several expensive cars. I was impressed.

"Make yourself at home, while I get us something to drink."

Pointing to the pictures, I asked, "You're a model?"

"Part-time to pay for my schooling. I'm studying to be a psychologist."

A light bulb turned on in my head. That explained her take on me. She returned with two glasses of wine and handed me one. We sat down on opposite ends of the couch.

"Nice crib," I said, not really knowing what else to say.

"It's home," Deidre replied.

I remembered her mentioning about walking in my shoes and asked her what she meant by it. A distant look glazed over her eyes as she told me how her fiancé, Tyrone, walked out on her a week before they were to be married and eloped with his cousin. On the scale of crappy things for a guy to do to you, this had to be worse than what Jeremy had done to me. However, everybody hangs on to their pain differently.

I drained my glass and set it down on the coffee table. When she'd finished hers, she got up and fetched the bottle from the kitchen. She sat down close to me and offered to refill my glass. I declined, already feeling warm and fuzzy. She filled hers and took a sip as she stared into my eyes. We were sitting so close now that I could feel the heat rising from her body. She touched my thigh and a spark of electricity shot though me. It was weird. On one plane, my brain registered she was a woman and screamed at me that this was messed-up. I'd never been with another female before and it was something I'd never thought would happen to me. However, I was as horny as hell. When she gently pulled my face close to hers, her breath felt warm and moist against mine. My heart began to race and my body was more than willing to go along for the ride. The alcohol worked like an aphrodisiac on me.

Our first kiss was as soft as a whisper and yet it sent the pit of my stomach into a whirl. The sensation of kissing a woman and the feelings it stirred up were different than I'd ever experienced before. They were pleasant and yet, weird, because she was a woman. I wasn't sure what to make of them—until the next kiss.

The second kiss knocked me for a loop. Deidre parted my lips with the tip of her tongue.

Once inside, she began to explore the inner recesses of my mouth. As her tongue made love to my mouth, I forgot she was a woman and teased it with my own. Each new kiss caused spirals of ecstasy to pass through me, awakening every part of my body. I wanted to keep kissing those soft sensual lips of hers. However, she moved her mouth slowly down the side of my neck and I heard myself moan.

Taking that as a green light to proceed, Deidre pushed me back on the couch and began to stroke my face tenderly as she kissed me. Then her hands dropped to explore my body. She cupped my boob through the material of my blouse. Even through the clothing, I felt my nipple tighten into a hard nub. At this point, I didn't care what she was. Because I'd never been with a woman before, I was clueless. Luckily, she sensed this and took the lead. Something told me she had lots of practice.

She opened my blouse, and I reached behind and unclasped my bra. This made her smile. Suddenly making her happy seemed very important to me. She bent down and sucked my tit, wrapping her tongue and lips around my tightened nipple as she kneaded my other one. I felt my heart begin to hammer inside my chest as my blood raced through my veins. Using her lips and mouth like a fine-tuned instrument, she licked and sucked my breasts until I was ready to explode. Then she stopped to unzip my jeans. That moment felt like forever. Wanting her to touch me, I shrugged out of them and my panties as quickly as I could.

My breath came in spurts as she gently worked her hands up my inner thighs. My hips involuntarily arced up toward her. She ran her fingers through the hair covering my mound. I spread my legs, opening up myself to her. I wanted to be touched—no—needed to be touched. She slipped a finger inside me, then another, and I rubbed against them.

"You feel so good, Sara," Deidre murmured as she continued to explore.

"Oh, yes," I managed to say, wanting her to continue. At that point, I would have sold my soul to have her caress me.

She kissed me hungrily, her almond eyes pools of liquid desire, as her fingers found my clit. Already swollen and hard, her touch sent my senses reeling. I felt on fire, melting from the inside out. When she replaced her fingers with her mouth, it nearly paralyzed me with a pleasure I'd never experienced with Jeremy. She licked and sucked my clit until I could hardly stand it much longer and yet I heard myself cry out, "Don't stop!"

On the edge, so close to coming, I grabbed fistfuls of Deidre's hair and ground my pussy into her face as she continued to stroke and like me like a kitten lapping up milk. When she pinched my nipple between her fingers, I screamed as I self-imploded, followed by one wave of pleasure after another. The intensity of my orgasm was so unreal. I'd never had one like this before.

I came back down to earth a very grateful camper, with my engine still revving. More than anything, I wanted to repay the pleasure. Pulling her up toward me, I ran my fingertips gently down the side of her beautiful face. Then I kissed her mouth, tasting myself on her lips. That kiss deepened as we tried to devour one another with our mouths.

Breathless, I pulled away and kissed my way down her neck as I began to undress her. The sight of her nakedness excited me nearly as much as I'd been moments before. Her breasts, small and firm, looked tasty enough to eat. Like a wide-eyed child let loose in a candy store, I straddled her, as I suckled and licked one nipple and rolled the other nub between my thumb and my forefinger. I wanted to touch and kiss every square inch of her. Deidre's soft moans and fingers stroking my bottom spurred me on.

Playing with my Barbie doll as a child was never like this. I loved how soft her skin felt as I ran my hands slowly down her back to her butt. I squeezed and released her tight bottom before running my tongue up the side of her tender thigh. She groaned and guided my hand to her pussy.

I'd never been so up front and personal with someone else's pussy before. Hers was so wet and warm. I easily slipped two fingers inside. Her pussy muscles tightened around them as she bucked and gyrated her hips to some rhythm in her head. A moment or so later, she half-moaned, "Eat me."

I removed my hands and split her pussy lips. They reminded me of the petals on a rose, as I unfurled it. Then I lowered my head and breathed in the musk of an aroused woman for the first time. It stirred my senses and I had this sudden desire to bury my head in Deidre's pussy and never come up for air. I slipped my tongue inside and tasted her. It was a strange sensation at first, but feeling her pussy muscles grip my tongue turned me on and made me wet. I began to tongue-fuck her, experimenting as I went along until she took hold of my face to control my speed. Grabbing her butt, I lifted her closer to me. I could not get enough of her.

"That's it baby, suck me. Yessss..."

She grabbed handfuls of my hair and massed her pussy against my mouth. I alternately licked and sucked her clit. Reaching up, I stroked her breasts. From her moans and quickened breath, I knew she was coming. She rocked against the couch, moving faster and faster, until she gave out an ear-piercing scream, drenching my face with her love juice.

Afterwards, we cuddled together on the couch with my head on her chest.

"Are you sure you've never been with a woman before?" Deidre asked me.

"You're my first," I replied, licking at her left nipple and watched it tighten.

"You're a natural then."

"So am I gay?" I asked.

"No, silly. Just liberal with your sexuality."

"That's an interesting way to put it."

"Come on," she said. "Let's go get more comfortable."

She got up, took my hand, and led me into her bedroom. It was done up in pink and red. I thought it suited her. She pulled the pink bedspread off and tossed it on a chair. Then she pulled me onto the crisp sheet and kissed me, stoking my passion, once again. Before long, we were loving one another again until exhaustion overtook us.

***

I woke the following morning with her tight, hot body wrapped around mine. I was now sober and began to feel weird about last night. As we sat having coffee, Deidre sensed I needed to talk.

"About last night..."

"Sara, it's what you want to make of it, nothing more."

I put down my cup and looked across the small, round kitchen table at her radiant smile.

"I know I enjoyed every minute and would love it to be the start of a relationship. However, if you're not comfortable being with me, that's okay, too."

"It's not that," I said, chewing on my bottom lip.

"What, then?"

"I'm not sure I know."

"Look, we don't have to rush into anything. We can get together as just friends and do things like dinner, if you like," Deidre suggested. "And if you feel like making love, we can do that, too. No strings."

"I'd like that," I replied enthusiastically. I had a terrific time last night."

Deidre gave me a wide grin. "So did I?"

That's how the two of us hooked up. The very fact, there were no strings seemed to bind us together and we've been pretty much a steady couple since that wonderful night. When I was with Deidre, I had no desire for a man. Whether or not I was gay wasn't an issue, only a label.

Jeremy was history. I never considered getting even with him. When I split, I wanted to forget I'd ever had feelings for him. Our last scene together wasn't pretty. I told him what I thought about his cheating ass, and slammed the door on him and our relationship. I never expected our paths to cross again. However, I soon learned to never, say never.

Deidre and I were having a quiet dinner at a steakhouse downtown when Jeremy walked in with an attractive redhead on his arm. She had a rack on her that had to be silicone enhanced. It got to the table a good minute before she did. I didn't detect their presence until they were standing in front of our table.

"What's wrong, Sara?" Deidre asked. "You look like you've just seen a ghost."

"More like a demon."

Before I could add anything more to my statement, Jeremy said, "Tsk, tsk. It's Saturday night and you're out with a girlfriend. Too, bad."

Deidre asked, "Do we know this asshole?"

"It's my displeasure to introduce my ex, Jeremy."

"Ah, Jeremy. Wasn't that the guy you left for *me?*" Deidre asked.

Jeremy's eyes bugged out of his head. He looked at me with undisguised shock on his face. "You...you left *me* for a *dyke*!"

People turned to look at us as I went in for the coup de grace. I didn't care about the

attention. He deserved what we were dishing out.

"What can I say? She's twice the man you ever were and always satisfies me."

Red-faced and humbled, Jeremy fled the restaurant with the woman in tow. Deidre and I laughed so hard we cried. Whoever once said that revenge was sweet knew exactly what they were talking about.

"That was beautiful, babe," I said, affectionately squeezing Deidre's thigh under the table. "Thank you."

"My pleasure. Glad I was able to do it."

The other diners went back to minding their own business after Jeremy left. That scene with Jeremy was a Master Card moment and truly priceless; a genuine Technicolor Kodak memory that would forever be etched in my mind.

Deidre and I went home to my place still hyped. We laughed about it some more before we ended up in bed.

"Hey, girlfriend," I purred. "Come *satisfy* me." Why not take advantage of a good thing, I mused.

Smiling, she replied, "With pleasure."

Making love with her that night lived up to the hype I'd given Jeremy. The world of love she'd taken me to was constantly growing. I never bored of her kisses or touch. She seemed to know how to keep me happy and I lived to please only her. If someone had told me a year ago that I'd fall in love with a beautiful, captivating woman, I would have laughed in their face. The thought that may have been absurd then was now my reality. When I planned something, I always did it around Deidre, who'd since become the center of my world.

Of course, I analyzed our relationship and wondered why it worked so well. Being a woman with another woman, we knew what turned each other on. No mystery, there. Only satisfaction, I thought as I ran my hand down the side of her smooth leg. She turned to kiss me.

Aside from loving, Deidre was so smart on many levels. She seemed to know what to say and do most of the time. And, no man, I'd ever know had as good a track record as she. When we first met, she hadn't made any demands of me. "No strings attached," she'd said. Knowing I was free to come and go as I pleased, I opted to stay. Deidre had wanted me from the start and had mentioned it, yet she wasn't clingy. The last thought occupying my mind before I fell asleep, was how lucky I was to have found her.

***

My sexy lover taught me so much about love and life in such a relatively short time. The biggest lesson of all was to never feel ashamed of your feelings or hold back. Like Deidre, I wanted to please her, as well, and tried to think of clever things to do to surprise or brighten her day.

One day I passed a bar with an unusual name. I decided to check it out and called Deidre.

She met me a half-hour later, in the parking lot of the Empty Sac. We kissed hello and went inside. Somehow through the smoke-filled haze, I spied an empty table. Like magic, a waitress materialized to take our drink order. Deidre grabbed a few pretzels from the basket in the middle of the table.

"They're fresh," she said in a surprised voice.

It took a few minutes more for my eyes to stop tearing. I wondered if they purposely kept the place dimly lighted to give it an intimate atmosphere or whether it was to save on the cost of electricity. When my eyes adjusted to my surroundings, I noticed there were people from several rungs of the economic ladder. There were men in suits, whom I expect came from work for a drink before heading home and laborers, still dusty. One man wore a leather jacket and nursed a beer next to his motorcycle helmet. There was a tattoo of a snake peeking out from the collar of his tee-shirt.

The waitress returned with our drinks. We sipped in silence a few moments and I continued to look around at the other patrons. I guess it was the writer in me that forever needed to be fed with details. I wondered how many people were there drinking the days of their lives away, trying to drown out their sorrows. In contrast, I was the happiest I'd been in a very long time. Deidre was, by far, the most beautiful woman in the place and I caught several men and even a woman checking her out.

Deidre began to play footsies with me under the table. Before long, her foot was inching up my leg. We both were wearing short skirts with no panties. It was our little secret. Fooling around like that made me hot. I could tell from the flush on her face that she was sharing my building lust. Soon, I was as horny as hell.

"Let's check out the Ladies' room," I suggested in a labored voice. Even breathing had become difficult.

We slipped out of our seats and hurried towards the restrooms. I grabbed her hand and pushed open the door. Eyeing an empty stall, I pulled her inside.

"Sara, what...?"

Her words were spoken into my mouth as I kissed her. I'd already had my hand under her skirt seeking her hot little pussy. The kiss deepened, our mouths opening wider and then wider still as our lust consumed us like wildfire. She ran her hand down my back and grabbed my tush as I raked urgent fingers through her hair. We rubbed against one another as I nuzzled her neck and tongue-fucked her ear. She purred as I slipped my other hand up her shirt capturing a tit. She was totally into this scene now and half-sat down on the john, resting one outstretched leg on the toilet paper holder. I got down on my knees and pulled her top off over her head. Her perky tits greeted me and I began to suck at one with sloppy gusto as I reached down to stroke her cunt with my other hand. My skirt had ridden all the way up and Deidre grabbed my ass. Her skirt had rolled up to look more like a belt than anything else. As I nestled between her legs, I breathed in the musky scent of her arousal deeply. Her pussy glistened with love dew. I lowered my mouth to her love snatch and licked her already swollen clit.

She pushed my face closer, practically burying it in her pussy. "Suck me, Sara!"

I rubbed her tit buds with my fingertips as I flicked my tongue up and down her opening, lapping at her pussy. Then I focused once more on her clit, licking it gently to tease and drive her wild, before I sucked and tugged on it with my lips. Her eyes half-closed with pleasure. She snaked her hands in my hair, using them as a way to control the speed and roughness of my strokes, which she tended to alternate. I thrust my tongue into her as deep as I could, squeezing her tits harder. Her body quivered, jerking spasmodically as if she'd just been electrocuted, as each pleasurable wave of her climax washed over her. She cried out as her love juice drenched my face.

After she'd finished coming, it was definitely my turn. I practically ripped off my blouse to free my boobs so I could rub my nips against Deidre's as she rose. We soul-kissed long and hard before I lowered myself enough to lean against the commode. I spread my thighs as wide as I could. Instead of going down on me as I'd hoped, she kissed me hard, thrusting her talented tongue deep into my mouth. I sucked on her tongue, feeling my juices begin to froth. She slipped her tongue down the side of my neck to my tits and teased them, pulling them with her lips until they were hard peaks, causing me to cry out. I began to squirm and begged her to eat me. However, she was hell-bent on torturing me first.

Deidre, ignoring my pleas, began to suck my earlobe while her hands slowly roamed my body. I raked her sweat-slicked back with my nails. Spreading my butt cheeks, she slipped a finger inside before doing the same to my pussy. Then she began to fuck me with her tongue as she slid both fingers in and out of my holes. Already wet and hot, I ground my love hole into her face. She began to nurse my clit. That was all I needed to send my body into pleasurable spasms. I moaned as she lapped up my girl-juice.

We embraced in one last tantalizing kiss before pulling our tops back on. As we opened our cubicle door and walked out, the door to the adjacent one opened and a short, heavy-set man came out. Our eyes widened to the size of saucers when we saw him zipping up. He had a contented smile on his moon-shaped face.

"Thanks, for the great entertainment," he said as he grabbed his crotch to emphasize what he meant.

We followed him out, and sure enough, there was a small icon of a man on the door. We'd been in such a hurry to get it on, that we'd missed it.

-The End-

PEEPING TOM

By
Candy Caine

Stripped down to my bra and panties, I was stretching on my den floor doing my yoga exercises. As a novelist, I believed limbering one's body also exercised their mind making them a better writer. Suddenly, I got the awful sensation that I was being watched. I could almost feel their eyes slowly slipping down my body as a feeling of violation rose within me.

Scrambling to my feet, I peered out the glass sliding doors, but no one was out there. I quickly slipped into my robe and stepped outside to look around more thoroughly. A lone crow standing on the picnic table cawed at me in disgust for disturbing him as he picked at a crumb. He seemed to be the only thing around. My house was a small ranch, in a cul-de-sac, surrounded on two sides by woods. And if that wasn't private enough, a solid six-foot fence ran the entire perimeter of the backyard. Could it have been my imagination?

Then I recalled I'd gotten the same eerie feeling last week while I was vacuuming the living room rug in shorts and a halter top. At first I thought I might be going crazy, perhaps losing the last remaining parts of a once sane mind—the obvious result of too many deadlines. However, this was the second time I felt violated in such a manner. But then, why would anyone want to watch me vacuum a rug or do yoga exercises? It wasn't as if I was doing it in the nude.

Strange, I thought, really strange. Even so, with this second incident, dare I write it off as the result of an overworked, feverish mind?

By the time my husband, Jay, came home, I'd forgotten all about the episode. It was our fourth anniversary and we were going out to dinner to celebrate. Jay had made reservations at the new restaurant on Johnson Avenue. He'd heard it served great seafood, which we both loved.

Our anniversary celebration couldn't have come at a better time. Jay and I desperately needed some quality time together. He'd been working long hours and I was trying to forge ahead with my writing career. Along with that, we'd reached an impasse in our relationship and boredom had settled in. We seriously needed something to spice up our sex life. Therefore, we were both looking forward to this romantic dinner and then, a well-deserved and sorely missed, good time in bed.

It's almost comical now, but nearly a month ago, I attempted to seduce Jay. Not willing to sit back and watch my marriage trickle down the drain, I decided to do something about it. I'd read, from cover-to-cover, a book on how to seduce your man and embark on an exciting sex-life. Following one of the suggestions I'd just gotten Jay into bed and disappeared into the bathroom for a minute. When I emerged dressed in my provocative peignoir, my red hair cascading down my shoulders, I intended to rock his socks off. Unfortunately, during the short time I was gone, Jay had fallen sound asleep. I was so frustrated that I didn't care if he was awake or not.

I stroked his balls with one hand while I took his flaccid cock into my mouth and sucked life into it. When it became hard, which didn't take long, I lowered myself down onto it and slowly began to pump up and down as I planted silken kisses along his chest. A huge smile appeared on Jay's face, but he remained asleep. Men are such remarkable creatures, sometimes.

Still in control, I continued humping his pole until I'd had an orgasm. Hey, it would have been nice if he helped a little, but who's complaining. At least I fell asleep satisfied.

For our special anniversary dinner, I'd gone shopping and purchased a seductive backless, black dress with a plunging neckline. It fit me like a glove and I'd hoped it would help whip Jay's juices into a lather. Perhaps Jay liked the dress a little too much, because when we were handed the menus, he tried to tell the waiter to skip the main course and bring us dessert.

Every aspect of the dinner was working out so well. The restaurant had lived up to its hype. The food was delicious and the portions large. We both had calamari appetizers and lobster dinners. Of course, the prices were just as grand, but this was a special night for us. We intended to enjoy ourselves and not worry about a thing. The waiter was quite attentive and kept refilling our wine glasses, compliments of the management in honor of our anniversary.

The wine had begun to have an effect on me. A warm glow was spreading slowly throughout my body and I simply loved how good it felt. Wantonly, I slid my shoe off and ran my toes along the inside of Jay's thigh.

"The alcohol has made somebody horny," he whispered, but the lopsided grin plastered on his face, I could tell he was enjoying its benefits, as well. Because I didn't want to wait until dessert was over and we could leave, I did something extremely impulsive. Since we were sitting in a booth side-by-side, I reached down and unzipped Jay's slacks. Reaching inside, I took Jay's cock out and began to stroke it. His eyeballs nearly popped from their sockets.

"What the hell are you doing, Jill?" he whispered.

"If you don't know by now—"

"You know what I mean."

"Nobody can see."

"That's not the point—oh, yeah," he groaned.

"Give me your napkin."

A moment later, it was over and Jay was sitting there with a huge smile on his face.

"Let's get out of here," I said.

Wanting to really make this a night to remember, we booked a room at a nearby motel. According to the self-help book, a change of scenery often spiced up the sex by making it more exciting. We figured the motel room would be perfect. Well, I certainly made it a night to remember.

Instead of awakening the next morning in the motel room with Jay by my side, I found myself alone in my own bed. Somehow I couldn't help but feel that whatever had gone wrong had been my fault. Unfortunately, though, I seemed to have no recollection of what happened after we left the restaurant. I remembered getting into the car, but virtually nothing else beyond that. I felt awful. Aside from a slight hangover, I felt guilty about ruining the evening.

The more I tried to remember, the more my memory tape played back blank. Being a fairly decent fiction writer, I came up with a working scenario. It starred me drinking way too much wine and conking out cold in the car. A disappointed Jay had decided to take me home. If anything like that had happened, I wondered if he'd come home from work upset, or worse—angry.

As a conciliatory gesture, I made Jay one of his favorite meals. I felt bad and truly hoped I'd be able to make the ruined night up to him. Being a terrible coward, I didn't dare call him at work to find out how he really felt. I could wait until he got home to find out.

After working myself up all day about Jay's feelings, he both surprised and relieved me by coming home in a good mood. When he discovered that I'd prepared shrimp scampi for dinner, he was thrilled.

Wanting to apologize for last night, I finally brought the subject up. "I fell asleep from all the wine I drank, didn't I?"

"The minute you sat down in the car and your head hit the backrest you were out like a light."

"I'm so sorry, Jay, for spoiling the evening."

"You didn't, Jill."

"I didn't?"

"Nah. I ravished you anyway, even though your snoring nearly drove me crazy."

"You're kidding, right?"

"Yup."

I shook my head. He really had me believing him for the moment.

"It's all right, babe. How many times have I conked out on you recently?"

"But last night was supposed to be a special one..."

"There will be others. So don't beat yourself up over it."

"As long as you're not upset."

"Shit happens. Forget it."

I certainly felt a hundred percent better after that conversation. Even so, I promised to try and make it up to him somehow.

It turned out to be a quiet evening. Jay had brought home some work from the office to finish and I completed another chapter in my novel. I soon became bored and went in search of my husband.

I found Jay, sitting at his desk, and slipped my arms around his chest as I nuzzled his neck. He looked up at me and smiled. I loved that boyish smile of his and no matter how many times he combed his black hair; it always had a rumpled sexy look, as if someone had just run their fingers through it. He pulled me down into his lap. His lips slipped down my throat, planting tiny, baby kisses along the way. I parted my lips and he thrust his tongue inside as his hands found their way under my top, unclasping my bra. Running one hand up and down my back, he took one of my nipples between his thumb and forefinger and kneaded it into submission. I heard my breath grow short as I felt a familiar pulling at my core.

Our kisses became passionate as our breaths became one. I unzipped his slacks and encircled the head of his cock. He pulled off my top and bra and fastened his mouth to my breast. We continued like this for a short time longer before he rose from his chair and carried me into the bedroom.

He laid me down on the bed and stepped out of his slacks. Just watching him take off his clothes took my breath away and I could feel my simmering love juices heat to a boil. He had a perfect cock, straight and thick. I removed the rest of my things and reached for him.

He dropped into my outstretched arms and kissed me as he began to slowly pay homage to my naked body with his hands and lips, lingering in every conceivable and inconceivable nook and cranny.

I was steaming, my passion well into the red zone, and wanted to feel him inside. "Now," I half-moaned.

He slipped inside, filling my pussy completely. Thrusting in and out slowly, he rubbed against my clit, allowing me to savor every long stroke of his magnificent cock. As if he were listening to my rapidly increasing heartbeat, Jay moved faster and began to pump into me until I screamed out in pleasure. He continued a few moments longer before he reached his climax. We collapsed in a heap, his head resting on my chest. I stroked his back and ran my fingers through his hair as our vitals slowed to normal.

Now that the urgency of the moment was over, Jay and I began to make love once more. Only this time we took it slowly. His lips sought mine and his tongue slipped into my mouth. My hand dropped to his cock and I stroked it back to life.

I slid down and took his growing erection into my mouth and began to suck as I tugged on his balls just the way he liked it. I heard him groan softly in pleasure. A moment later, he motioned for me to turn around on my side so he could service me as well. As I licked and sucked at his shaft, his tongue probed and licked inside me. Only moans and groans could be heard at our suck fest as we pushed each other over the edge. Sated this time, we both drifted off to sleep.

***

The following evening Jay had a surprise for me. On the way home from work he'd stopped at Great Videos and picked up a skin flick to get us in the mood. What a marvelous idea. After last night, why not make tonight just as exciting? The anticipation of having more great sex had me creaming in my pants. At this point, I was willing to try anything to keep the momentum going. Besides it being a win-win situation, I still felt a tinge of guilt about ruining our anniversary celebration.

Jay helped me do the dishes after dinner so we could get to the movie faster. I wondered if he feared I'd fall asleep. I couldn't blame him if he did. Sometimes, I'd be watching a movie on TV with him and conk out.

I'd seen porno movies before, but this one had a real plot and held our interest. We really got into it and before long; we were putting our own spin on the plot as we reenacted the script. We couldn't get out of our clothes quickly enough. Once the cotton barriers were removed, Jay began to feast upon my body, teasing one breast and then the other with his sensual lips and tongue doing what he did best. The exquisite torture nearly drove me to distraction. He parted my thighs and slipped two fingers into my wet pussy. Slowly he moved them in and out. My tight muscles closed in around them.

I sought his mouth and he kissed me as our tongues did an impromptu dance for dominance. He slipped his cock into me and we rocked together this way for a short time before we slid to the floor.

I got to my knees doggy style as Jay moved behind me and slipped inside. Grabbing my ass, he pumped his cock into me, slowly at first. Within moments, he was hammering into me as I edged closer and closer to an orgasm.

It was hard to hear my moans of pleasure over his grunts. I could tell by his breathing that he was just as close to coming as I was. A beat later, I could feel the pleasure radiating out from within me. Then I felt Jay's body grow momentarily rigid knowing he'd come, as well.

"Baby, that was beautiful," he said, as we cuddled together on the rug in the den. The moonlight streamed into the room bathing us in a blue-white light.

As we lie there, Jay drew lazy circles around my breast. After a few minutes, I warned him, "You better stop that."

"Why? What's going to happen?" he asked.

"I'm going to get horny again?"

"Yeah?"

"Yeah," I said, as I pulled him over me.

As Jay straddled me, I could feel his cock hardening. He slipped inside me easily, filling me slowly and then pulling out just as slow, teasing me. This excited me. He continued to do this until I begged him to go faster. I threw my legs over his shoulders so he could penetrate me more deeply. He began to knead my nipples. That took me over the edge and my entire body convulsed in one long orgasm, followed by short aftershocks.

I have to hand it to Jay. He was right. Watching the movie did add something extra to our lovemaking—something explosive—like dynamite. It had been like our first time together all over again, but better.

The next day I was still hot, just thinking about the great sex Jay and I'd had the night before. It was hard to believe that I had gotten so turned on by an x-rated movie. I couldn't remain focused on my writing for more than ten minutes at a time. Instead my mind would wander and I'd get horny recalling Jay's hands touching me. I felt like a live wire ready to spark. There was no way I could wait until he got home so I grabbed my vibrator and got off. It slaked my appetite for a short time, but I soon found myself staring at the clock again counting the hours until he'd be home. This was definitely unlike me, but I found that I welcomed the change. It would be a very long time before I tired of the kind of sex we'd had last night.

By the time Jay finally arrived home I was more than ready to jump his bones. As he walked through the door I totally lost control. I was all over him, grabbing at his crotch and giving him a deep, longing kiss. He dropped his attaché case and asked, "Does my baby need some of my good loving?" as he nuzzled my neck driving me crazier.

"Mmm," was all I could manage at that point because I was too busy pulling at his clothing and biting his earlobe. He grinned and swept me off my feet. I was grabbing at anything I could reach and didn't care where we were heading. We actually made it as far as the den rug. The bedroom was too far away.

We practically ripped the clothes off each other's backs again. I couldn't believe how aggressive and wanton I was behaving. It was as if my body had been possessed by another woman. And Jay seemed to like it, too, because he was so hard.

"Baby, what have you been doing all day? I've never seen you this hot," Jay said, his voice labored and thick with passion.

"Thinking about us last night," I barely managed to say.

"We've got to do that more often," he said, as his mouth sought mine.

"Now would be just fine."

I was lost in a spiraling of sensation. Time and the outside world were all but forgotten as Jay had begun to run his tongue up the inside of my thigh. I knew where he was heading and my body seemed to do everything it could to get him there quickly. My moaning seemed to spur him on. Jay slipped a finger inside me and moved it in and out slowly, leaving a trail of my own juices which he began to lap up with his tongue. He then proceeded to make love to my pussy, alternately sucking and nipping at my clit. Slipping a finger into my ass brought me closer to the edge. I bumped and ground my pussy into his face as he continued to torment me with such sweet pleasure. Finally, my body was wracked with one wave of ecstasy after another.

After Jay finished pleasuring me, I pushed him down on his back and lowered myself onto his waiting rod. He reached for me and our mouths met as I began to move up and down, savoring every stroke my clit made against him. He cupped my breasts and closed his eyes. Our bodies, in total sync, moved to our choreographed rhythm. Pleasure began to build within me again. I could feel it pulsing from one end of my body to the other. I closed my hands on top of his wanting him to squeeze my nipples. That was all I needed to take me over and I exploded into a world of vivid colors. He joined me in paradise. The aftershocks continued for what seemed to be a delightfully long time.

The sex we had just experienced was just as incredible as the night before. As we lay spent, cuddled on the rug in the afterglow, I gazed out through the glass sliding doors. Suddenly a momentary reflection of light caught my eye. I bolted upright to a sitting position.

"What's the matter, honey?" Jay asked.

"I thought I saw something...There look! There's someone out there by the fence."

"Yes, you're right! I see the reflection of light hitting his glasses."

Jay went closer to the sliding glass doors and peered out a minute before the guy realized he'd been seen and moved out of sight. "I think it's that weird guy from across the street , with all the cats."

I wondered if he'd been watching me the other times. It probably was. "Jay, I think he's been watching our house."

"Yeah, I can see that."

"No. I don't mean just tonight."

"You mean he's watched us have sex before."

"I don't know about that, but there were a couple of times when I felt someone was spying on me."

"Doing what? You haven't been giving your business to anyone else have you?" jay asked raising an eyebrow.

"Of course not, silly. I was vacuuming."

"Now that's a turn-on if ever there was one."

"Is he pathetic, or what?" I asked. Then as an afterthought, "Do you think he's still there?"

"I just saw him duck."

"Yuck! Let's close the blinds."

Jay smiled mischievously. "Let's not. If he's still there, let's give him something to see that really knocks his socks off."

"Are you out of your mind?" I asked, blushing and embarrassed by the thought of having someone watch Jay and me make love. I was far from being a prude, but I was hardly an exhibitionist.

But when Jay started to kiss me, my desire took hold and I soon forgot all about the crazy guy outside.

After we had finished making love for the second incredible time that night, Jay said, "Perhaps we should leave the blinds open all the time. That was the greatest."

"Only if you promise it will always be this fantastic. Too bad we can't share the wonderful way I feel now with everyone."

"Why, not?" Jay said.

"Why, not, what?"

"Share with everyone."

"Okay, that's it. This is where I draw the line," I said and we both broke into laughter.

"Is that guy still there?" I asked, peering out through the glass. "I can't see him."

"Nah, he's gone. Maybe we bored him to death."

"I doubt it. Don't you dare suggest a re-run just in case, though."

"Baby, that would be impossible. I'm worn out, but maybe..."

"Forget the maybe," I said, kissing him. "Tomorrow will be soon enough."

"That's exactly what I was going to say."

"I'll bet."

"I guess he hit the jackpot tonight."

"Who?"

"Our neighbor, the peeping Tom."

"So did I, Jay," I said, sliding my arms around his neck and pulling him close.

Now that Jay and I had discovered the way to reenergize our sex life, we were also able to find more quality time to be together again. It was almost as if we had turned the clock back to when we were newlyweds. And I loved every fantastic moment. I intended to do everything in my power to make sure we didn't fall into the marriage doldrums again.

***

Several months later, I scanned the cable program guide to see what was on. I couldn't believe it. With so many different TV channels listed, there wasn't one decent thing to watch. We had already seen all the movies and programs worth watching. I began to wonder if I'd seen reruns of the reruns.

Jay came into the kitchen and asked one of his two favorite questions of the evening, "What's on the tube tonight, Jill?"

"Nothing. *Absolutely* nothing. We've seen everything worthwhile."

"That's great. What else is new?"

"Maybe we should rent a movie," I suggested.

"Why? Is my baby in the mood?" Jay asked with a wicked little smile.

"I was referring to a regular movie, sweetheart."

"Too bad," he said, teasingly, as he nuzzled my neck. "I would rather be bad to the bone tonight."

I chuckled at his clowning. "I'll get my coat."

We rented two movies. I picked up a copy of Casablanca, which I was in the mood to see again. I could never get enough of that romantic movie. Jay picked up a porno flick, just in case, of course. Whatever it was, it had taken him close to twenty minutes to choose it.

We watched Casablanca first. Surprisingly, I wasn't at all tired when it ended and was more than willing to watch some of the movie that Jay had selected. It was the least I could do since he had agreed to let me watch mine in its entirety.

"Why don't we watch it upstairs in our bedroom? That way if I fall asleep I'm already in bed," I said, laughing at my own cleverness.

"With such stimulating company, there's no way you're going to fall asleep," Jay asserted.

I put a serious expression on my face and said, "In that case I'll make every effort to stay awake."

"Just make sure that you do," he said, propelling me up the steps into our bedroom.

He popped the DVD into the player. We both leaned back on the bed and got comfortable. The title flashed across the screen. I laughed when I saw it. It was called: I Was a Peeping Tom. Now I realized why Jay had selected it.

"Interesting title," I said.

"I'm glad that you approve," Jay answered with that crooked little smile of his that I loved. "After our encounter with our nutty neighbor, I'd thought it would be a real goof."

I kissed him on the tip of his nose.

The screen went black a moment. When the picture came back on, we saw a house which looked familiar. Before I had a second thought about it, the camera zoomed into the house. I now knew why the house looked so familiar.

"Oh, my God! Jay! That's us!"

"How the hell...Our weird neighbor! He must have filmed us that night months ago. I was only kidding about what I'd said. I never really meant that we should become exhibitionists."

"I know," I whispered, still in shock and hoping this was all just a bad dream. "Jay, what if someone we know rents this movie?"

"Perhaps they'll learn something? Did you catch some of that great technique?" he said, patting himself on the shoulder.

"Jay!"

"Only kidding—but not about the great technique."

"What'll we do?"

"Pray that this is the only copy."

"And if it isn't?"

"Maybe we can embark on new careers."

"You're crazy."

"You've got that right. Crazy in love with you, and if that flick doesn't prove that, nothing ever will," he said, taking me in his arms.

"I love you, too."

"So what about the new career? I think I'll change my name to Slick Eddy with the big dick.

I began to laugh.

"What part of that did you find funny? It better not be the last half."

I couldn't stop laughing and he soon joined me. We laughed until the tears came. The whole situation was so outrageous. Besides, looking on the bright side, it would make a great story, which was the last thing on my mind before Jay began to make love to me.

-The End-

TOUCHÉ

By
Candy Caine

I love my wife. And I'm not just saying it in order to convince myself. No matter what I've done or will do in the future, I will always love Carrie, my long-legged, blonde, blue-eyed beauty. To me, she's the epitome of womanhood—my own very Venus, tall with all the curves where they're meant to be and the most perfect breasts I've ever held or tasted. My very own beacons to light the darkest of my nights. Sex with her has always been fulfilling and I consider myself quite a lucky man. However, as content and happy as I am with Carrie, there is a part of me that I keep hidden from her.

Every Thursday, while Carrie thinks I'm working late, I'm actually with Margo. Who might that possibly be you ask, since I have professed such undying love for my wife? Margo. How does one describe her? Well, she's half she-devil, half-siren, but all tigress. She makes me sizzle and fills a certain need in me. Her hair, the color of flame, is long and thick, while her eyes are green and all-knowing, not unlike those of a panther.

I never know what to expect when we meet. Margo tends to be mysterious and always has some new, exciting adventure planned. And when I fear she has finally out-done herself, she comes up with some totally outrageous scenario that leaves me breathless and completely in awe. Take last Thursday, for instance.

We had tickets to the theatre. Margo gave me explicit instructions to wear my trench coat.

"But, according to the weather report, there's no chance of precipitation throughout the entire week," I protested, not wanting to have to drag the coat around if it wasn't necessary.

"Jeremy, *I* know better. Trust me and *wear* the coat."

Knowing my phenomenal mistress had something up her sleeve, I did as she commanded.

The play was a revival of MY FAIR LADY and the theatre was packed. I took off my coat, folded it, and placed it on my lap. Margo, looking ravishing as usual in a clingy, short red dress that left nothing to the imagination, smiled and took my hand in hers. Halfway through the first act, she abandoned my hand and began to rub my prick. I had stopped wearing underwear on Thursdays long ago and felt her touch through my lightweight slacks as if she were directly touching my skin. In practically no time, she proceeded to drive me wild. Needless to mention, that I walk around every Thursday half-hard just thinking about meeting Margo later on. I held the coat just so to obstruct the view of the elderly woman on my left. I'm certain had she witnessed what we were doing she would have had a stroke. Margo unzipped my slacks and unleashed my rigid tool and continued to stroke me.

Moments later, Margo whispered into my ear, "Don't come yet. Hold your coat over your cock and follow me."

We rose from our seats together and made our way out to the lobby and into the men's room. I had some reservation about this, but luckily the bathroom was empty. Choosing the furthest stall from the door, she sat down on the toilet and took my entire cock into her mouth right down to the shaft as she tugged on my balls. Within seconds, I let loose a jet of cum. In an attempt to swallow it all and not miss a drop, Margo wrapped her talented tongue around my spent cock and licked it until it glistened only with her saliva.

I started to zip up my slacks, but Margo stopped me and purred, "Haven't you forgotten me?" as she took my hand and placed it on her wet pussy.

"But how—?"

"Come on, quickly," she said in a voice dripping with excitement, as she half-dragged me from the stall.

A moment later she was sitting on top of the counter by the sink.

"But what if someone comes in?" I asked nervously glancing at the door.

"They can watch."

The thought of being caught in the act, breathed new life into my cock and by the time she had reached inside my slacks, I was ready for her. Her short dress had risen over her luscious, milk-white thighs revealing her clit and moist snatch. Feeling how wet her pussy was, I guided my shaft into that glistening cunt of hers. She let out a low moan as I slowly filled her. I grabbed her hips, drawing her closer. She began to rub her clit as I slipped my finger into her anus the way she liked. It was at that moment I thought I heard the door open.

Suddenly a voice behind me said, "Man, this fucking show is better than the one on stage."

That did it. I felt Margo stiffen. She began to moan as her vulva convulsed. From the corner of my eye, I saw a guy take out his member and began to jack off furiously.

"Would you like to finish me off, little lady?" the stranger asked.

Margo merely gave out a throaty laugh as she hopped off the counter. "Looks like you're doing just fine without me." Then turning back to me, she said, "Hmm. Now that I've had dessert, I'm ready for some dinner."

We linked arms and walked out of the men's room laughing.

Unlike my unpredictable girlfriend, my wife, Carrie, was a conventional lover. She was modest to the point of being shy. In fact, undressing in front of other women often gave her the willies. I could never picture her doing any of the outrageous things that Margo has done. You can't imagine how often I'd wished Carrie to be more daring and less inhibited. Like for instance the time we went to a movie a few months back.

Carrie and I were sitting in a darkened theater. I had draped my arm loosely about her shoulders. When I began to stroke one of her tits with the tip of my finger, she pushed my hand away.

"Why?" I whispered.

"Someone might see."

Poor Carrie was always so caught up in how people might perceive her. Because of this, she rarely displayed any form of affection in public. I blamed this on her cold fish of a mother who probably caused her husband to jack off to *Hustler Magazine* in the bathroom for relief.

Margo and I often talked after having sex. She was quite intelligent and we discussed virtually everything. Had she been born at an earlier age, she would have been a most delightful courtesan. During one of our post-coital conversations she asked me if I had any fantasies.

"I do have a fantasy and often think about it."

"Tell me about it," she said propping her head on her left elbow.

"I long to be part of a ménage a trois."

"Really?"

"Are you surprised?"

"No, not at all. I have often thought about it myself."

I couldn't help but smile at that. We were so in tune. Wouldn't it be wonderful if Carrie felt the same way?

"And do you have a fantasy?" I asked.

"Yes. I want to be stranded on some faraway island with ten well-hung, handsome men."

She must have seen the doubt on my face, for she laughed. "Oh, Jeremy, my sweet, you're included, of course." And with that she straddled me, rubbing her pussy against my cock, as she began to tease one of my nipples with her teeth. I felt a surge of desire rise within me as my cock awoke from its short nap.

Margo nestled herself down on me and began to move up and down like a well-oiled piston. I drew her closer so that I could suck on her luscious tit as I split the globes of her ass. She loved when I stroked the tender area between her pussy and ass. As the fire of pleasure built within me, her gasping breaths told me she was close. I slipped a finger into her ass and set her off. Seeing and hearing her delight, I let myself go and filled her. She collapsed into a sweet heap on top of me. I could feel her heart rapidly beating against my chest. I wrapped my arms around her slender back feeling quite content.

*****

It was four months later and I had quite forgotten my discussions of fantasies with Margo. She had left a message on my cell phone one morning. I smiled when I saw her number, remembering that Thursday was approaching. I called her back.

"Yes, my sweet," I said.

"Hello, my love. Meet me at the Vincent Hotel, room 216, Thursday night at 8:30. I have a most intriguing surprise for you."

"Really? Won't you give me a hint?"

"Then it won't be a surprise. All I can say is that it will be a night you'll *never* forget."

I could feel my groin responding to her words. She'd never disappointed me before. After hanging up with her, my mind raced through several different scenarios as I wondered what was in store for me. The anticipation was overwhelming that I could hardly wait for the following evening.

By the time I got home that night, I was still aroused. I had stopped to pick up a bottle of chilled wine for dinner. Carrie greeted me at the door and I handed it to her.

"What's the occasion?"

"A tiny celebration of my love for you?"

Her large, blue eyes twinkled. "I didn't know we needed a special occasion for that."

"Actually, we don't. I just felt the wine would be a nice touch," I said taking her into my arms and kissing her.

During dinner, we sat opposite each other. Carrie sipped her wine as she kicked off her shoes and got more comfortable. I noticed a wicked little smile form on her face as she began to stroke the inside of my thigh with her toes. They rose higher until they reached the tip of my cock.

"Is my honey, horny?" I asked.

"More than you can imagine."

"What would you like to do about it?"

"Slow dance."

I got up and walked over to our CDs and selected one from our *make-out* collection. A moment later, music filled the room and Carrie was in my arms, her lithe body molded to mine.

We began to move to the music. My attention was drawn to her pelvis pressing against my hardness. I cupped her bottom as she fitted herself around me. Her hair smelled like a bouquet of freshly-picked flowers. I tiptoed my fingers through it. I felt her wetness through her summer shift and panties underneath. I lowered my mouth and began to kiss the heaving tops of her breasts.

Reaching underneath her dress, I slipped a finger into her panties and teased her clit. She moved her bottom around it, obviously desiring more. To accommodate her, I slipped her panties down and she stepped out of them. We continued to move to the music.

I unzipped her shift so I could free her breasts and fastened my mouth on one. A moment later she pulled away and stepped out of her dress. Her hands fumbled with my zipper and she released my aching cock. I backed her up against the sitting room wall and lifted her onto my rigid cock. I hammered into her. She twisted her fingers in my hair.

Her breaths were nearly gasps as I felt her body begin to convulse. She moaned in pleasure and I came, shooting warm jets of cum into her.

Carrie smiled contentedly as she slipped her slender arms about my neck.

"I love you, darling," I said, meaning every word.

She smiled knowingly.

***

I knocked on 216. Margo whipped the door open, clad in a sheer flowered robe. She was wearing a mask. Had she not said something, I would have recognized her by her hair, just the same.

"Why the mask?"

"To heighten the pleasure. Sex with a stranger, the ultimate fantasy."

"But, I already know it's you."

"True. However, you don't know the third member of our ménage a trios," she said handing me a drink.

My heart leapt. She had remembered my fantasy. And in her own clever way was putting an exciting spin on it.

She led me into the dark room lit by only a candle on either side of the bed. Stretched out on the king-sized bed was her matching book-end. Another long-legged woman with black hair was dressed in the same manner.

Margo interrupted my thoughts. "I want to establish certain ground rules."

"All right..."

"First. Don't try to remove the other woman's mask. Don't try to engage her in any form of conversation, either. She's not going to talk to you. Secondly, you've got to obey my commands. Do you think you can go along with that?"

I nodded.

"Good," Margo said. "Let the game begin!"

A moment later the other woman joined her and together they removed all my clothing, ignoring my stiff rod that greeted them both. They pushed me back on to the bed and proceeded to tie my wrists to the bedposts. My pulse began to race. Could they hear my heart beating?

The women divided my body up according to some imaginary line. They began to plant kisses up my thighs, their lips and tongues working in unison, driving me crazy. I longed to touch them, but when I tried my constraints only tightened. They met at my cock and shared it by licking and stroking it with their tongues. I was fully aroused.

Jealously, I watched as their tongues touched and they began kissing each other. I wanted to be a part of it and yet, they ignored me. Margo slipped the robe off the other woman's shoulders. Her breasts were large and luscious with nipples that begged to be suckled. Margo teased one into a firm bud with her tongue as she fanned the nipple of the other. I felt like a voyeur, spying on them and my mouth went dry. My cock ached as the mystery woman sighed. She in turn opened Margo's robe and stroked her breasts, one at a time before slowly running her tongue over each nipple. My prick twitched in envy. The two women had become lost in each other, seeming to forget about me.

Margo stood and let her robe drop to the floor. The other woman did the same. They both climbed naked onto the bed and kneeled facing one another. Arms about each other, they began to kiss, tonguing each other as their kisses became more passionate. I was nearly hypnotized by their show, which I came to realize was all for me. And I was enjoying every blessed, but torturous moment.

Margo lay back and the other woman began to tongue her glistening cunt, teasing her clit as she reached up to touch her breasts. Margo slipped two fingers into the other woman's pussy. I watched as she gyrated around it. It wasn't long before Margo climaxed and they switched positions.

I feasted my eyes on the spectacle that had unfolded before me. My cock had remained painfully rigid the entire time and desperately needed some attention. I feared it was merely going to be a coupling and not a threesome.

Finally, the two women remembered that I was in the room and shifted their attention to me. The mystery woman began to suck my cock as Margo held on to the backboard and lowered herself over my face. The smell and taste of her juices was intoxicating and I found myself lapping it up like a hungry puppy.

I exploded in the mystery woman's mouth almost immediately and she sucked my prick dry nearly the same time that Margo came and covered my face with her love juice. Finally the women released me from my restraints.

Feeling like a child let loose in a candy shop, I was finally free to indulge. The stranger's body was pure poetry. She had long silky limbs that met at a smoothly shaved pussy which glimmered in the light. I buried my head in her hot snatch. Margo took my flaccid cock and began to breathe new life into it.

I rolled over on my back. The woman took my cue by kneeling over my mouth and tongue. This gave Margo room to lower herself down onto my rejuvenated tool. With her incredible muscles she was able to snap her snatch tightly around me and rode me as if I were an Arabian stallion. I was surprised at my own response, for I could feel another climax building.

They say "timing is everything". Perhaps the three of us gave new meaning to that old adage, for we all seemed to explode within moments of each other. The stranger above me threw her head back as her breath was broken into long shuddering pants. When she did that I thought about Carrie. Suddenly feeling guilty, I swept that thought from mind.

Margo had already gotten off of me and was pouring wine into three glasses. The other woman had slid down my chest and gazed up at me.

"You were wonderful," I said. "Thank you for joining Margo and me tonight."

"You're welcome," she said, turning on the light before she slipped off her mask and black wig, shaking her full head of long blond hair.

I gasped. It was my own wife, Carrie!

-The End-

I WAS IN LOVE WITH MY SISTER'S HUSBAND

By

Candy Caine

I'd just taken off my nurse's uniform and slipped into comfortable sweats when I heard a knock at my front door. Looking through the peephole, I saw Wayne, my sister, Amber's, hot- looking husband. He was holding Ty, their eight-month-old son in his muscular arms. How I wish those strong, powerful arms were holding me. I felt my own heart flutter slightly as I opened the door, something it always did whenever Wayne came around.

"Just get home, Rochelle?" he asked after stepping inside my apartment.

"A few minutes ago. What's up?" I asked as Ty grabbed my forefinger with his chubby little hand and cooed. Smiling, I leaned over and kissed the top of the baby's head.

"Sorry to bother you, Rochelle, but we're out of milk again and I have to give Ty his

bottle."

"Amber out working late again?"

"Uh-huh. That girl took off the second I got home." "I hope this new job she's got is good paying."

"Me, too. Especially with all the long hours she's been putting in."

Odd, I thought. What kind of job had my sister, who was hardly able to hold on to one in the past, rushing out to as if her very life depended upon it? "Here's the milk. If you need anything else just holler."

Our fingers briefly touched as I handed Wayne the milk. A delightful sensation flowed straight through me to my very core. I tried to mask the emotions I was feeling by reminding myself he was my sister's husband and could never be mine.

I'd thought when Amber got married she'd straighten up and fly right. She'd snagged the most wonderful guy in the entire world, the one man I truly ever wanted. And if he were my man, I'd make it my business to be home every night to keep him happy and satisfied. My little sister had to have a few loose screws to behave the way she did. She treated that man like dirt. If she didn't watch out, she was going to lose him one day.

We said goodnight, and I watched Wayne walk back to his apartment. Again I thought how my little sister better start taking better care of her husband. He was too prime to lose.

***

Nearly a week later, my phone rang at eleven o'clock. I was about to make myself a soothing cup of herbal tea and crawl into bed with a hot romance book.

"Rochelle...it's me, Wayne. I hope I didn't wake you."

"No. You sound upset. What's wrong?"

"Something's wrong with Ty—"

"I'll be right there," I said, hanging up the phone. I threw a raincoat over my nightie, grabbed my keys, and rushed out the door. My sister and her family only lived two doors down. I'd found them the apartment after she'd gotten married and needed a place to live.

As I knocked on the door, I could hear Ty crying. Wayne was pale and wore a worried look as he gingerly handed his son to me. "He's been this way for more than an hour."

"Where's my sister?" I asked already knowing the answer as I carried my nephew into his room to check him out on his dressing table.

"Working," Wayne said, following close behind me. "Lately, that's all she does. I think she's forgotten she has a baby to care for."

At this hour? It was difficult to work in my raincoat, so I took it off forgetting that I was in a nightie. I'd feared at first that it might be his appendix; however, it turned out that Ty was only very gassy and needed a good burping.

"Wayne, relax. It's not serious. Ty's only gassy."

"That's a relief. Is there something you can do to make him more comfortable?"

"I've got to get some of the gas out of him. Did you burp him after he had his bottle?" "Sure. I always do."

"Well, he's still got a great deal of air trapped inside that little body of his and that's what's making him uncomfortable. Can you please hand me a towel to put on my shoulder?"

Wayne disappeared a moment before coming back with a small towel and handed it to me.

"Here you go."

"Thanks." I placed the towel on my shoulder and held Ty upright against my chest with his head resting on the towel in case he spit up. Gently, I patted his back and was rewarded with a little burp. It wasn't enough. He didn't have to start fussing and fretting again for me to realize he was still very gassy.

Poor Wayne looked so worried and watched what I was doing closely. I lay Ty on his back on the dressing table again and began to move his pudgy little legs in a gentle bicycling motion; slowly pushing one leg up near his chest and pulling it back while pushing the opposite leg up to his chest. I repeated it several times as we listened to the alternate noises of the baby's bodily functions. Between his burping and farting, he cracked us both up. Finally, Ty seemed comfortable enough to be able to sleep. That was about the same time my sister came breezing through the door as if she hadn't a care in the world.

Amber was dressed as if she was coming from a dinner date and not work. One look at me and she was on the offense. "Do you always entertain my husband in a nightie when I'm not home?"

Feeling embarrassed, I grabbed my raincoat and struggled into it as quickly as I could.

"Ty wasn't feeling good and Wayne needed help."

"Sure. So you came running over *dressed for bed*," she said in a sarcastic tone as she tapped the toe of her red high-heels.

I wanted to grab her and shake her for so many reasons that my head spun. She looked like she'd just been out on the town and not working...unless she had the kind of job that I didn't want to put a name to. That would certainly explain the late hours. "Why are you acting this way? *You* should have been here for your child not me," I said, and left as quickly as my feet could carry me, feeling embarrassed as if *I'd* done something wrong.

What had happened to the sweet kid she used to be? The two of us used to be so close. I guess things between us began to fall apart around the time my mom was killed in an auto accident. I was eighteen and Amber, fifteen. She began to get into trouble—doing stupid things like smoking in the girls' room at school and shoplifting. She'd become a handful, and I feared she'd end up in jail or worse if I didn't get her off the streets.

Finally, I convinced her to take a job in a local supermarket as a cashier. It was there she'd eventually met Wayne. He was an assistant manager. They began to date and she ended up pregnant. I figured now that she was married with a child, she'd hang up her party shoes for more sensible ones and take care of her family. However, I could see that she hadn't. And what made things worse was that she was hurting a wonderful guy who didn't deserve it.

I knew it was wrong to have feelings for Wayne, but lately it was getting harder and harder to fight them, especially when he and I were thrown together more and more. Sometimes I found myself wondering how he felt about me. Secretly, I'd hoped he longed for me, as well, even though I knew it would be wrong to nurture any feelings between us.

Her treatment of Wayne wasn't the only thing that Amber did which bothered me immensely. She'd often borrow things, like clothing, and never bring them back. Then when I wanted to wear a particular blouse or skirt on a date, I often found it was missing. Most of the time, it turned out to be something that my sister had borrowed ages ago and not returned. Take my black knit skirt, for instance. One of the doctors at the medical center I worked in had invited me to a dinner party. I figured that it would be the perfect thing to wear to the party. When I looked in my closet for it, it wasn't there. Thinking back to the last time I saw the skirt, I remembered Amber had borrowed it ages ago and hadn't returned it. I nearly stormed over to her apartment to get it. Since it was Saturday, I expected her to be home.

Wayne answered the door. His handsome face broke into a grin when he saw it was me.

"Hi."

That smile warmed me inside and out. "Is my sister here?"

"No, she's out."

"Damn!"

"What's wrong?"

"I needed back a skirt she borrowed."

"For tonight?"

"Yes."

"Well, why don't you come in and see if it's in her closet? Ty's napping so I can help you look."

I followed Wayne into the bedroom and opened Amber's side of the closet. Without warning, shoeboxes came hurling out like guided missiles narrowly missing my head by inches.

"I guess your sister isn't a regular Suzie homemaker," Wayne said and we laughed together.

"I guess some things never change. Sharing a room with her was always an adventure. I never knew what I'd be walking into. Wait! I think I see my black skirt."

"Be careful. Those other boxes up there don't look too steady," he said only a second before they, too, came tumbling down forcing me backward into his arms.

Our eyes met and locked a moment before his mouth gently covered mine. The small taste of his sweet lips wasn't enough for me. I needed more and found myself kissing him back with all the pent up passion I felt. Then reality stepped in and I pulled away. "We can't do this," I said between breaths.

"But you want me. And I need you."

"This is wrong. You're my sister's husband."

But Wayne either didn't hear my protests or care. Instead he moaned my name into my hair as his hands gently caressed my face and neck, sending currents of desire through me. His lips seared a path down my neck. I could no longer resist as his lips sought mine once more. His hand fondled my breast through the fabric of my blouse. I could feel my nipple harden as he bent his head and gently nipped it with his teeth. My moans drowned out the small voice in my head pleading with me to stop. Wayne opened my blouse and kissed the rising swells above my bra. I reached around and released the catch so he could suckle my breast. Though I wanted that man more than I could say, I tried to apply the brakes to what seemed to be a runaway train.

As Wayne pulled me closer and I felt his hardness against me, I whispered breathlessly,

"What about Amber? What if she—"

He placed a finger across my lips. "She won't be home till after dinner," he said as he swept me off my feet and on to the bed.

I knew this was so wrong. What we were about to do was unforgiveable. Yet, I felt compelled, caught by a wave of passion and determined to ride it wherever it took me. He slid off my jeans and panties in what seemed like one fluid motion. I watched transfixed as he stepped out of his jeans. His manhood, thick and large, was ready for me. I don't know how many times I had fantasized about this moment and now it was actually coming true.

I took his hand and pulled him down to me. His lips captured mine and his tongue made love to my mouth leaving me breathless as he parted my thighs and gently inserted two fingers. I rubbed against his fingers and moaned once more. I desperately needed to have him inside me. To complete and make me whole, I thought.

As if reading my mind, Wayne nudged the gentle folds of my sex open with his manhood and slid slowly inside, filling me completely. Our bodies began to move in unison. Every pleasurable stroke took me one step closer to heaven. Before long the pace had quickened and we climaxed together in each other's arms. It had been as wonderful as I'd envisioned it to be.

Lying in his strong arms afterwards, I came to my senses thinking about the consequences of what we'd done. "We must never let this happen again, Wayne."

"Why? I'm not sorry it happened. And I *doubt* if you are, either."

I shook my head. "What we did was wrong. You're still my sister's husband."

"In name only, Rochelle."

"What do you mean by that, Wayne?" I asked, hearing the ominous sound of his words.

"We hardly sleep together, lately. I can't even remember the last time we made love."

I looked into his sad dark eyes. How could Amber not desire to sleep with that incredibly sexy man who had just fulfilled my every desire? Was she crazy?

"I think she's tired of me—bored is a better word."

"Why do you say that?"

"Because she'd rather be out working than home here with me. And lately you've been more of a mother to Ty than she has."

"Have you tried talking to her?"

"Yes, but do you see her? She blows in and out of here as if the apartment had a revolving door. Obviously she couldn't care less about me or Ty."

"Sometimes I don't understand my sister. Perhaps you two should go see a marriage counselor."

"I doubt if she'd go. She obviously thinks everything is fine just the way it is."

I shook my head in wonderment. "I'm so sorry."

"I'm not any longer," he said, stroking my cheek.

"It doesn't change the fact that we mustn't do this again. If Amber found us in bed together..."

"Let her!"

"No. It would hurt her."

"And what about me? Don't you think I'm hurt by the way she's been acting?"

"My sister's a fool."

"Besides, I'm in love with you."

I got very still when I heard that. I'd always wanted to hear those words spoken by him, but not this way. It was wrong—so very wrong. My tears began to fall as I murmured, "No, please. Don't make it worse." I grabbed my things and hastily put them on, despite Wayne's pleas for me to stay a little longer. I knew in my heart that I wanted that man more than I've ever wanted any other man, but I made a solemn promise that I wouldn't allow what had happened between us to recur again while he was still married to my sister.

For the next week or so I tried to avoid Wayne. I hoped that time might lessen our feelings and desire for each other. I couldn't have been any more wrong.

I even went on a blind date, something I ordinarily would never, ever do. Emmy, a maternity nurse that I'd known for several years fixed me up with her brother. Ray was a nice- looking, sweet guy with a great sense of humor. Even though he was fun to be with, he wasn't Wayne. The problem was that I compared every man I met with Wayne. And it was no different with Ray.

"Rochelle, you're exactly as my sister described you," Ray mentioned over quiet dinner in a Chinese restaurant downtown.

"Is that good or bad?"

He gave out a short chuckle. "Finishing for a compliment, are we?"

"I'll take them from wherever I can get them."

"Okay then. Here's a compliment for the lady: good. However, I do believe you've got something weighing mighty heavily on your mind."

"Why do you say that?"

"Because part of you is just about a million miles away."

"I'm so sorry, Ray."

"Is it another man?"

"You're beginning to freak me out. Are you clairvoyant?"

"No." He smiled. "Only observant. I glimpse such sadness in your eyes."

"To be honest with you, I have feelings for a married man."

"I know it's probably none of my business, but I've been there and done that. I can assure you there's no future in it."

"I'm well aware of that."

Ray smiled and then said, "But since when did good advice ever stop anyone from taking a bumpy ride on love's merry-go-round, learning from first-hand experience."

"I wish we'd met at a different time in my life."

"Me, too. I think we could have started something really nice."

I smiled and touched his hand. He took my hand, raised it to his lips, and kissed it. Our eyes locked for a long moment before he called for the check.

Getting into bed later I thought about Ray. He was a sweet, sensitive man with a good job, definitely the right type of person I should be with instead of someone married to my own flesh and blood. I imagined him to be quite the romantic, never forgetting a woman's birthday or an anniversary. But, despite all those fine qualities, he paled in Wayne's shadow. No other man could possibly fill Wayne's shoes or the part of my heart that he owned. Damn! Why couldn't I forget Wayne?

I missed seeing Wayne. Even though I purposely stayed away, I still wondered how he was feeling. I truly hoped my sister opened her eyes and began to appreciate the treasure she possessed. I closed my own imagining our lips locked in a passionate kiss as Wayne stroked my body into a frenzy with his long fingers. Then Ray's words of caution came back to me and I questioned why I choose to torture myself.

The following evening Wayne knocked on my door. Ty was with him.

"Can I speak to you a minute, Rochelle?"

I opened the door. Ty wanted me to hold him. I took him in my arms and gave him a kiss on his cheek.

"Would you like some coffee?"

"Yes."

I took out the portable playpen I kept in the closet for those times I babysat and put my nephew down within it. When the coffee was ready, I set it down on the table. It was difficult to control my overwhelming desire to kiss him. However, Wayne took charge of the situation. Before I could react, he took me in his arms and kissed me. I tried to protest and push him away, but my resistance was too weak. His tongue pushed its way into my mouth and took possession. His hands caressed the planes of my back sending jolts of pleasure through me. Despite my desire to continue to kiss him, I pulled away.

Releasing me, he asked, "Why have you been avoiding me?"

"To prevent something exactly like this from happening. I meant what I told you that Saturday afternoon. We can't be committing adultery."

"We belong together."

"You belong to my sister."

"I can't continue to perpetrate the mistake I made."

I sunk down into my chair as Wayne took my hand in his. There were tears in his eyes. I felt my own heart respond.

"The truth is that I married your sister simply because I made her pregnant. And after having said that, the ironic thing is, though I love him, I now doubt that Ty is even my child."

I couldn't believe what Wayne was telling me, and I was too speechless to interrupt.

"Amber was a party girl and a great deal of fun to hang around with, but I never loved her. When she introduced me to you, I knew you were the one woman I'd always wanted—the one person I'd been destined for. The night I was going to break off with her and ask you to dinner, she told me she was pregnant. I thought I was the only guy she was hanging with, but I found out differently later on from someone she'd been sleeping with, as well."

Tears began to slip from my eyes. Wayne kissed them away. "I've been in love with you for so long, Rochelle. I often tried to imagine how wonderful it would be to make love to you. When it finally happened, it was every bit as terrific as I'd dreamed it would be and more. Staying away from me is almost like taking away the very air I breathe. Especially now that I know you feel the same way about me."

"Wayne, I'm not my sister. I know right from wrong. While you are married to Amber, I must stay out of your bed."

"Is this what you want?"

"It's the way it must be."

My heart was breaking in two as I watched Wayne take Ty home. Despite my honorable intentions, I heard a tiny voice inside my head calling me a fool. That night I cried myself to sleep.

***

A few days later, I bumped into Michelle, a sweet maternity nurse who I'd gone to school with. She looked wonderful. I guess being a newlywed can do that to you. After we talked a few moments about each other, she asked me a strange question.

"Did your sister divorce that cute husband of hers already?"

"No. Why do you ask?"

"Because the other night I saw Amber in a lounge drinking with a guy who definitely didn't look like the person you introduced me to in the supermarket. Not unless he's been pumping steel and shaved his head."

"She works at night now. Perhaps it was an innocent drink between her and her supervisor or maybe even a new client."

"I'd love to have a supervisory relationship like that," she replied nearly smirking.

"Why? What was she doing?"

"She was practically giving this guy a lap dance. And his hands were nowhere in sight."

What could I say to Michelle? Unfortunately the more she continued, the more uncomfortable it made me feel. Amber had lied when she told Wayne she was working that night. I grit my teeth and thought; she was working all right—working hard at cheating. And what about the other nights?

"Look, I have to run. It was nice bumping into you, Michelle," I said as I fled down the hall.

How long had my darling sister been cheating on Wayne? Had she never stopped her partying ways at all? I had to admit, when it came to Amber, anything was possible. Not that her terrible behavior excused what had happened between Wayne and me. That was still wrong no matter how you looked at it, but it certainly did make our crime less terrible. It also explained why she hadn't needed to sleep with Wayne. She was taking her business elsewhere. Again, I wondered, what the hell was wrong with my sister?

I was very angry—no furious— with Amber. She was hurting the one man I cared deeply for and couldn't have. Wayne was a good person and didn't deserve such betrayal. I wanted to run to him and tell him about her infidelity straight away. However, my head told my heart it would be wrong and nixed the idea. Why hurt him even more with such awful news. No. I couldn't do that. Wayne would have to find out about Amber on his own. I only hoped it was sooner rather than later. In her own selfish way, Amber was playing havoc with all of our lives. That in itself was so terribly wrong.

The next evening, Amber walked into my apartment as cool as ever. I found it difficult to keep my tongue.

"Rochelle?"

"In the bedroom." I was folding laundry. And at that moment, the last person I desired to see was my sister.

"I need to borrow a blouse to wear with this skirt. I spilled wine on mine."

I wanted to ask if it really was wine. With little stretch of the imagination I visualized how she might have soiled her blouse. I tried to remain quiet, but heard myself ask, "Need it for work tonight?"

"As a matter of fact, I do."

That's when I lost it and blasted her with both barrels.

"Come off it, Amber. What kind of job has you out at all hours of the night in clubs entertaining men?"

"What are you talking about?" she asked through narrowed eyes.

"Were you working the other night when a nurse from the hospital saw you at Devine's?"

"Of course."

"Doing what? Giving lap dances?"

"Rochelle, I don't have to explain myself to you."

"Maybe. But how about Wayne?"

"You didn't tell him, did you?" Her face paled.

"No. Wayne's a good man and deserves better."

Relief quickly spread across Amber's face, but soon changed to annoyance. "And of course, *you* would know," she insinuated.

At that moment I found myself hating her. How did she always seem to make me feel bad?

"Look, give me the blouse. I'm late."

I handed it to her, wondering how she could hurt Wayne so easily without any shame or guilt. As I watched her walk out of my apartment, I realized she hadn't even thanked me.

I couldn't sleep and could hardly eat. Knowing that Amber was cheating on Wayne was killing me. If he were mine, I'd never leave his side for a moment, let alone, deceive him with other men. Eventually I knew Wayne had to find out what my charming sister was up to. I couldn't help but think that he must have his suspicions already.

***

A week later, Wayne got a phone call from a very angry woman claiming to be the wife of Amber's lover. At first, he thought she was some kind of crazy calling the wrong number and hung up on her. However, when she called back with more damaging evidence, Wayne knew the woman was speaking the truth.

I'll never know how he didn't immediately confront Amber when she came home later that night. Instead, he decided to find out the truth for himself. The next evening after Wayne came home from work; he called me and told me all about the phone call he'd received from the angry wife. I wanted to rush right over to his apartment to console him, but comfort wasn't what he sought from me. In fact, he had something quite different in mind.

The following evening when Amber left for work, Wayne followed her while I watched Ty. Remaining a safe distance behind her, he followed her into an apartment building. She got off the elevator on the fifth floor, but there were twelve apartments on that floor. There was no way for him to figure out which one she had entered, so he was forced to wait for her to come out and confront her then. As he waited, he told me his fury grew. By the time Amber emerged from the building, he was ripping mad. Because he didn't want to get into a "he said-she said" situation in court when he applied for a divorce, he taped what happened next.

"Amber!"

"Wayne! What are *you* doing here?"

"Unfortunately, I *know* what you're doing here."

"What's that supposed to mean?"

"Don't play stupid with me. Did you think I'd never find out?"

"I...I..."

"Wondering how I knew about this place?"

"Rochelle told you?"

"Your sister had nothing to do with this."

Sobbing, Amber said, "I'm so sorry."

"Not as much as I."

"Can you forgive me?"

"No. You've never been a good wife or even a decent mother."

"What are you going to do?"

"Do I have to paint you a picture? I want you to clear out of the apartment by tomorrow night."

"But where will I go?"

"Go back to wherever you just came from. I don't care what you do."

When he got back to the apartment he was still shaking in anger. I'd never seen him this angry.

I listened to the tape. When Amber began to sob it hadn't been because she'd been remorseful. She wasn't sorry for any of the hurt she'd caused. Knowing her, she realized she was caught and tried to use tears to wiggle out of the net. It would seem that Amber didn't care that she'd been caught cheating or was about to lose her son one bit. All she cared about was having a place to stay. Deep down inside I was happy Wayne threw her out. She truly deserved every bit of his wrath and then some. I was in love with him and this would bring him a step closer to me. However, I realized that I had to be patient and wait. If he really loved me as much as I cared for him, our time would eventually come.

The following evening my sister banged at my front door as if she wanted to knock it down. "Where were you?" she demanded as I opened the door.

"At work."

"I know that. You should have been home an hour ago."

"I stopped at the supermarket. What's up?"

"Don't be cute. You know Wayne threw me out."

I nodded.

"I need a place to stay until I can get on my feet."

"You can't stay here. I'm not getting involved between the two of you."

"But you're my sister!"

"I know and I love you, but—"

"Whatever happened to blood being thicker than water?" she asked.

Before I could respond, her eyes became narrow slits and she spat at me. "It's him, isn't it?"

"What?"

"You're in love with Wayne."

I began to reply, but she continued, "You told him to leave me because you wanted him for yourself. I've always known it."

"Listen to yourself. You're ranting. Sure I care about him. He's a great guy, but I had nothing to do with the breakup of your marriage."

"Yeah, sure. Tell me another one, sis."

"This is not about *me*. *You* cheated on Wayne and hurt him. And Ty? Have you given any thought to him?"

"Yeah, Wayne can keep him."

I looked at her in disbelief. What kind of mother was she? Hell, she didn't even sound human.

"Don't look at me like that. Bill hates kids."

"I take it Bill's your lover. You're willing to walk away from Ty because some guy doesn't want him. What happens if things don't work out between you and Bill? What happens if he decides to remain with his wife? You will have lost everything for nothing."

"I don't need this shit," Amber said and stormed out of my apartment.

I watched as she raced down toward her own apartment and took her key out to open it. I couldn't help but smile when it didn't work. Wayne had the super change the locks.

Amber rapped on the door. "Open this damn door, Wayne. I know you're in there."

When Wayne finally allowed her into the apartment, I closed the door. Amber was probably grabbing her things. I had no idea where she'd go now, nor did I care. She had turned into some terrible creature I hardly recognized.

Wayne asked me to come with him when he went to speak to a divorce lawyer. I agreed.

It was a simple process. Amber would receive a summons to appear in court. It could get sticky if my sister decided to contest it, but Wayne had the tape proving Amber was an adulteress and would play it in court, if necessary. However, my sister never even bothered showing up. The judge granted Wayne the divorce and complete custodial rights—not that he worried Amber would challenge him for Ty. She hadn't been a mother to the boy from the start. I had gone to court with Wayne for moral support. We both left that courtroom relieved and extremely happy.

***

"I'm a free man," Wayne said, taking my hand in his as we sat close together in a corner booth at an upscale restaurant in the Royal Hotel, celebrating the night his divorce had been finalized. We had left Ty with a neighbor in the building and drove into the city for a quiet celebration dinner.

"Yes, you are," I replied, feeling the happiest I'd been in a long time.

"Will you marry me, Rochelle?" he asked.

I put down my glass of champagne and gently stroked the side of his handsome face. "There's nothing in this world that would make me happier, but are you certain you want to jump from the frying pan into the fire? After all, you just got divorced today," I teased.

Wayne grinned and lowered his face close to mine. "Uh-huh. That's true. However, I'm ready to jump in feet first."

He covered my mouth with his. The kiss sent sparks throughout my body as I began to anticipate the pleasure that was to follow. Signaling the waiter, he motioned for the check.

A moment later, the waiter placed the leather check folder on the table. Wayne opened it and studied the bill a few seconds before slipping his credit card into the binder and handing it back to the waiter. When the waiter returned with the credit card receipt and a pen, Wayne added the tip and signed.

"Thank you, Sir," the waiter said.

"Let's go upstairs," Wayne said.

We walked toward the elevator holding hands. The doors opened and we stepped inside an empty car. Wayne took me into his arms and kissed me. By the time the elevator reached our floor, we were both breathless. We got out of the elevator and walked to our room. He slipped the key card inside the slot and the green lights lit up. Stepping inside, the door had barely closed behind us before I was back in his strong arms, once more.

We kissed our way over to the bed. Falling back on the bed with our lips still locked, I could hardly believe any of this was actually happening. My heart was careening against the wall of my chest as Wayne slowly began to undress me. He removed my silk blouse and kissed the rising swells of my breasts, aching to be released. A moment later, my bra was tossed aside and Wayne was suckling my nipple. My restless hands tugged at his belt.

Wayne stood and opened his belt, then his slacks and stepped out of them. Next he opened his shirt and off it came. His cock, pushing through his boxers, looked primed and ready for me. Without taking my eyes off of his beautiful body, I stepped out of my skirt and panties. He took his boxers off and rejoined me on the bed.

In one forward motion, I was in his arms. Wayne reclaimed my lips, crushing me to him. His tongue sent shivers of desire racing through my body. I returned his kiss with a hunger that I'd kept pent up inside of me for so long. When his lips left my mouth to kiss my neck, mine felt as if they were on fire. My senses practically short-circuited as his lips slipped down from my neck as he kissed his way to one breast and fanned the other with his fingertips. I raked his back with my nails as I felt him place one finger, then a second into me. It was as if I were melting from the inside out.

I wanted to feel his cock inside me now. I arched my back and lifted my body. My love juice was pooling around Wayne's fingers. He removed them and nudged his engorged cock into me. I gasped in pleasure as he lifted me into his lap. Holding my hips, he moved me up and down his love stick. I licked his ear and kissed his neck as I felt an orgasm building within me. It was getting closer and closer with each stroke. I let myself go with abandon and cried out.

"That's it baby girl, let go," Wayne said, as he lowered me to the bed and pumped into me until he reached his own climax.

Drenched in sweat, we both collapsed in a heap. Wayne rolled over and took me into his arms. Holding me tightly, he kissed my face, my eyes and finally my lips.

"I love you, Rochelle."

"I promise never to let you out of my sight," I replied.

He smiled down at me. "I'm a very lucky man."

"I never thought you'd ever be free. You have no idea how much I prayed for this day."

"But do you know what the best part is, Rochelle?"

I looked into his warm brown eyes and shook my head.

"We have all the time in the world and the rest of our lives to share."

-The End-

ABOUT THE AUTHOR:

With nearly 200 short stories, several novels and novellas in print, hot and spicy, Candy Caine keeps her husband, Robert, on his toes in their Arizona home. Supportive with her writing career, he's always willing to help her make certain the scenes in her stories are authentic. After all, technique is so important for good writing. When asked why she began to write, Candy says: "I've always loved books and my biggest thrill is to bring the joy of reading to others. That's what writing is all about.

Be sure to check out Candy Caine's other titles.

Dancing for Dollars
    For the Love of Money
    Honor Most Profane.
    Justify My Love
    A Bridge to Love
    Forever in my Heart
    That Summer
    Because of You
    Save the Last dance for Me
    Crazy Love
    Softly As I Leave You
    Flavor of the Week
    For Your Love
    Heated Pleasures
    More Heated Pleasures
    Peek into the World of Candy Caine
    Short Stories Created by Candy Caine
    Chasing Rainbows
    The Life and Loves of Ariel Jones
    At First Sight
    No Strings Attached
    Overboard